You Were Mine

ALSO BY ABBI GLINES

In publication order by series

The Rosemary Beach Series
Fallen Too Far
Never Too Far
Forever Too Far
Twisted Perfection
Simple Perfection
Take a Chance
Rush Too Far

The Sea Breeze Series
Breathe
Because of Low
While It Lasts
Just for Now
Sometimes It Lasts
Misbehaving
Bad for You
Hold on Tight
Until the End

The Vincent Boys Series
The Vincent Boys
The Vincent Brothers

The Existence Series
Existence
Predestined
Ceaseless

You Were Mine

A Rosemary Beach Novel

Abbi Glines

ATRIA PAPERBACK

New York • London • Toronto • Sydney • New Delhi

ATRIA PAPERBACK

A Division of Simon & Schuster, Inc.
1230 Avenue of the Americas
New York, NY 10020

This book is a work of fiction. Any references to historical events, real people, or real places are used fictitiously. Other names, characters, places, and events are products of the author's imagination, and any resemblance to actual events or places or persons living or dead is entirely coincidental.

First Atria Paperback edition December 2014

ATRIA PAPERBACK and colophon are trademarks of
Simon & Schuster, Inc.

For information about special discounts for bulk purchases, please contact Simon & Schuster Special Sales at 1-866-506-1949 or business@simonandschuster.com.

The Simon & Schuster Speakers Bureau can bring authors to your live event. For more information or to book an event, contact the Simon & Schuster Speakers Bureau at 1-866-248-3049 or visit our website at www.simonspeakers.com.

Interior design by Dana Sloan
Cover art © Stephen Carroll/Arcangel Images

Manufactured in the United States of America

10 9 8 7 6 5 4 3 2 1

Library of Congress Cataloging-in-Publication Data is available.

ISBN 978-1-4767-7607-1
ISBN 978-1-4767-7608-8 (ebook)

To every reader who has lost someone they loved.
May your heart find its own healing through
unconditional love.

Prologue

Tripp

Everyone has that defining moment in life. That one choice you have to make. I had my moment, and it has haunted me ever since. In those defining moments, you either pave a road to happiness or you regret every step from then on. For me, I don't know which road would have been the best, because between my two choices, neither of them included *her*.

I was young and so fucking scared. Scared of being forced by my parents to be someone I didn't want to be. Scared of making the wrong choice. Scared of leaving her. But mostly, I was scared of losing her.

She was my regret. Leaving her changed me. The moment I climbed onto my bike and drove out of Rosemary Beach, Florida, I left true joy behind. I'd only had that summer with her, three months that altered me forever. But what I would never be able to forgive myself for was that they had changed her just as much. She was beyond broken now. I couldn't reach her.

Seeing her in pain broke my soul. Losing my cousin Jace had caused deep pain in both of us, something I never wanted to relive. He would forever be in my heart. I'd never forget his

1

laugh and the easy way he loved and lived his life. He didn't live in the world of fear I inhabited. He chose his path, and he walked it. He was the better man. And I had been able to stand back and let him have her. She deserved the better man.

Now he was gone, and both of our worlds were thrown off-balance. Because I couldn't stand back anymore. No one was protecting her. No one was holding her, but she wouldn't fucking let me near her. She wasn't going to let me fix the past. I'd severed any hope of that when I'd driven away and left her with no other choice but to be with Jace.

If only I could embrace the emptiness and accept it. But I couldn't. Not when I saw her lost, beautiful face. She needed me as much as I needed her. Our story wasn't over. It would never be over. If I had to stay here and watch over her, even though she wouldn't let me get near her, I would. For the rest of my motherfucking life. I'd stay right here. Making sure my Bethy was OK.

Tripp

Eight years ago

It wasn't just another summer. It was my last summer here in Rosemary Beach. I was already feeling the suffocating presence of my father and his plans for me. He was so sure I'd leave for Yale in the fall. I'd gotten in, thanks to his connections. He'd made me take a tour of the campus, and once I was in, he'd forced me to accept. "Nobody turns down Yale." It was all that ever came out of his mouth anymore. Yale this, Yale that. Goddamn Yale.

I wanted to be on my Harley. I wanted another fucking tattoo. I wanted to feel the wind in my hair and know I had nowhere I had to be. That life was free. I was free. Before this summer was over, I was going to ride off without a word. Leave behind the money and power that came with being a Newark and find my path. This wasn't my world. I would never fit in here.

"Hey, sweetie, I didn't see you walk in," London Winchester said as she slipped her arms around one of mine and held on. That was another reason I had to get the fuck out of here. London. My mother was already planning our wedding. Didn't mat-

3

ter that I'd broken up with her last month. London, her mother, and my mother all believed I was just going through a moody phase or something. My mother said it was OK if I needed to sow some wild oats this summer. London would be patient.

"Where's Rush?" I asked, glancing around the house full of people. If Rush Finlay was throwing parties again, then his mother and his younger sister, Nan, had to be out of town. Rush owned the place. His father was the drummer in the legendary rock band Slacker Demon. His mother and his sister benefited from all the money Rush had, thanks to his dad. Rush's mother had been a groupie once, and although Rush's dad, Dean Finlay, seemed to care about his kid, he didn't give a shit about Rush's mom. They had never married. Nan had another father, who was also out of the picture.

"Outside by the pool. Want me to take you to him?" she asked sweetly. That sweet tone was so fucking fake it was ridiculous. The girl was venomous. I'd seen her in action.

"I can find him," I replied, shaking her loose and walking away without a backward glance.

"Really? This is how you're going to be now? I won't wait around on you forever, Tripp Newark!" she called out after me.

"Good," I said calmly over my shoulder, then headed into the crowd, hoping to get some people and some distance between us. I'd been with her for two years. She'd been a really good fuck, and once I thought maybe she was it. But I could never actually say I was in love with her. This past year, I had realized I was simply tolerating her. I dreaded seeing her, and when I faced the facts, I realized I was keeping her around to make my parents happy. But I was done with that. No more keeping the parents happy. I was keeping *me* happy.

"Tripp!" Woods Kerrington called out from a circle of girls surrounding him. He was such a fucking Romeo. He made them all believe they had a chance.

Holding in a chuckle, I nodded my head in his direction. "What's up."

"Hopefully a lot of things real soon," he replied, and this time I laughed. "Jace is outside with Rush and Grant if you're looking for him."

"Thanks."

Jace was my younger cousin, and Woods was Jace's best friend. I'd had them both in my life for as long as I could remember.

Turning through the crowd, I headed for the back door.

"Stop it! I said no, Jonathon. I'm not interested."

I stopped in my tracks. That didn't sound good.

"I got you in here tonight, and I'm not getting any thanks for it?" The guy was angry and sounded like a prick.

The girl didn't respond right away. I moved toward their voices and stopped outside the kitchen. I recognized the Jonathon guy the girl was talking to. He was a tennis instructor at Kerrington Country Club, which was owned by Woods's family. He was also a notorious asshole and had fucked most of the cougars in town. If he was about to take advantage of this girl, then I was going to throw his ass out.

"I just . . . I didn't know . . . I want to leave." The way the girl's timid voice cracked told me she was scared.

"Fuck that, bitch. I don't care how damn hot your tits are. I'm not dealing with this shit. You can find the door by yourself," Jonathon snarled.

I took a step toward the door as Jonathon stalked through it. Stupid little fuck.

I shoved him back into the kitchen with one hard push. He was going to apologize for being a dickhead before I threw him out. I doubted Rush even knew he was here. Jonathon wasn't in our circle of friends. Some of the cougars he had slept with included a couple of our mothers. Not on our favorites list.

Getting his sorry ass to apologize would do him some good. Poor girl should have known better than to mess around with the help at the club. Maybe she'd learn a lesson after this.

"What the fuck?" he shouted, and then his eyes widened when he realized who I was. My dad sat on the board at the Kerrington Club, and I could have Jonathon fired with one word. He knew it.

"That's what I was wondering, Jonathon. What the fuck? What the fuck are you doing at Finlay's house, and why the fuck are you treating your date so badly? She too young for you? I know you prefer the over-forty crowd," I said, taunting him. I wanted him gone. Just one wrong move, and that was all I needed to make sure he lost his job without feeling a shred of remorse.

"I didn't . . . I mean, I was invited. I got an invite. This is just a girl whose aunt works at the club. She's not anybody."

Glancing over at the girl in question, I recognized her right away from her big brown eyes. She was Darla's niece, Bethy. I'd seen her before. Hell, it was hard to miss her. Jonathon was right about her tits. They were noticeable. But her sweet face and innocent look had kept me from moving in on that. Besides, Darla was scary as hell. She handled hiring the employees at the club, and she'd been there forever.

"Bethy, right?" I asked her.

Her big eyes got even bigger before she nodded.

"This guy's a douchebag, sweetheart. You shouldn't trust him. Be careful who you let take you out."

"You know her?" Jonathon asked incredulously, as if she were too beneath me to notice.

Stupid shit was getting on my last nerve. I turned my attention back to him. "Yeah. I know her aunt. The woman who hired your sorry ass. I wonder how she'd feel if she knew how poorly you were treating her niece?"

Jonathon's fear was obvious. He had a good gig at the club, and he didn't want to lose it.

"Leave. Don't ever come back. Finlay finds out about this, he'll do more than give you a warning. He'll beat your sorry ass. He likes Darla. We all do. Stay the fuck away from her niece."

Jonathon turned his attention to Bethy. The furious gleam in his eyes was directed at her. She shrank farther back, putting more distance between them until her back was pressed to the wall. Dickhead was getting off on scaring her.

Stepping between the two of them, I glared at Jonathon. "Leave. Now."

I could tell it was taking everything he had to keep his mouth shut, but he did. I watched as he muttered a curse and turned to leave the kitchen.

"Make sure you don't stop until you're off this property," I called out after him.

When he was gone, I turned back to Bethy. She was wringing her hands and looking nervous. I'd gotten rid of the prick. Why was she upset now?

"You good now?" I asked her.

She bit her bottom lip, then shrugged. "I, um, don't know."

She didn't know? I couldn't keep from grinning. She was

pretty damn cute. But she was young. "Why don't you know?" I asked. I enjoyed the way she talked. Her voice was husky but sweet.

She let out a small sigh and dropped her gaze to the floor. "He was my ride. I don't live close by."

As if I would let her get back into the car with that fucker. He had to be four years older than her. He was older than me. "I'll give you a ride. I'm safe. Jonathon isn't. Besides, he's way too old for you. Dude would go to jail if he touched you."

She lifted her eyes back up to look at me. "I'm almost seventeen," she said, as if that were legal, although she was a little older than I expected. She was so expressive. I liked that. She didn't try to bat her eyelashes or pucker her lips to look sexy. She was real. How long had it been since I'd been with a girl who was real? But then, she was young, and she'd been raised in a very different world from mine.

"Yeah, sweetheart. But he's almost twenty. He shouldn't have gone anywhere near you."

She looked deflated, then nodded. Surely she hadn't wanted to stay with him? Fuck that, what was Darla teaching this girl?

"I'm sorry I ran him off, but he wasn't treating you right."

Those eyes went wide again, and a dimple appeared in her cheek. "Oh, don't apologize for that. He wanted me to go back to a bedroom and uh . . ." She trailed off. She didn't need to explain. I was pretty sure of what he wanted to do back in a bedroom with her.

"Come on. Let's get you home," I said, nodding toward the door.

Bethy

Ohmygod, ohmygod, ohmygod, Tripp Montgomery, or was it Newark—I wasn't sure; I'd heard him called by both names—was speaking to me. He was actually looking at me and talking to me. It was hard to breathe. When he'd shoved Jonathon back into the kitchen, looking like an avenging angel, my heart had gone into a frenzy.

He was the most beautiful man I'd ever seen. I was ten when I first saw him at the club. I'd been trying to load the drink cart for Aunt Darla because she was mad at me for running around outside in front of members instead of sitting in her office until she finished a meeting. So I thought if I helped her, she'd be happy again.

The problem was, I couldn't carry the cases of drinks because they were too heavy, so I'd carried four single drinks at a time from the cooler to the cart. It'd been ninety degrees outside, and after five trips, I was getting exhausted. I'd let my attention wander and ended up tripping over a step and dropping all the bottles of beer in my arms. Glass had shattered everywhere.

I was sure that Aunt Darla would never let me come back and stay with her. I'd be stuck with the stinky old neighbor lady in the apartment next door who yelled at me all the time when Daddy was working. And he was always working.

Tripp had walked up and seen my mess. Without a word, he'd started cleaning it up. I'd stood there in awe of him in his khaki shorts and white polo shirt, looking like a teen model in a magazine. When he'd glanced up at me and winked, my ten-year-old heart was lost.

That had been our last interaction, although I'd been watching him from afar all these years. He was my favorite daydream. Now here he was, saving me again.

I followed him as he walked out of the kitchen. When he saw the large crowd of people gathering in the living room, he reached a hand back and took mine. Any ability to breathe was now gone. Tripp Montgomery Newark was touching my hand. He was holding it. If I died today, it would be OK. Because of this moment, my life was now complete.

He weaved his way through the crowd, holding my hand in his. People called out his name, and many looked at me curiously when they saw him pulling me behind him. I didn't know what to do with the attention. These were people I'd watched my entire life, but they'd never acknowledged me.

"What are you doing?" London asked in a horrified voice, just as we pulled free of the people. This was not good. Tripp and London had been a couple for years. Everyone knew it. When I'd heard he'd ended things with London, I'd been so happy I'd smiled like an idiot for a week. Which was silly, really. It wasn't like Tripp was going to realize I was alive now that London was out of the picture.

"Leaving," Tripp replied without looking at her.

"You're leaving? With her?" she asked, even more horrified.

Tripp let my hand go and opened the front door. "Yep" was his only response.

"Who is she?" London asked, looking furious.

"That's not your business," he said, then looked at me. "Come on, sweetheart."

He was calling me sweetheart again. I was seriously close to swooning. Right here on this marble floor.

"Tripp, do not walk out that door!" London warned as he opened the door and stood back for me to walk through. I quickly stepped out before London decided to take a lunge at me.

"Ignore her," he whispered as I walked by.

It was like we had a secret. I shivered.

He closed the door on London, who was talking nonstop, and let out a sigh of relief. "Damn, she's exhausting."

He didn't seem like a man upset over a breakup. That was good. I couldn't think of anything to say to him that didn't sound stupid. I wished I had some witty insight to make him want to be around me.

"Ever ride a bike?" he asked, stopping in front of a motor-cycle. I knew he drove a Harley. Everyone knew it. But I hadn't thought about getting to ride on it with him. This night was just getting better.

"Uh, no," I replied, trying to keep the absolute giddiness from showing on my face.

"I'll be your first. Sweet," he said, then winked at me.

My heart stopped. Tripp had winked at me. I'd been so worried about tonight. I hadn't been sure about Jonathon, but I'd wanted to see how the other half partied. I'd heard all about it, but I'd never been. Never had I imagined that I'd hold hands with Tripp, that he would wink at me, that I'd get to ride on the back of his bike. This night was going to be the most epic of my life. I was sure of it. "OK," I managed to say without stumbling over the word.

He grinned, and it was perfect. I loved his smile. He handed me a helmet. "Put this on," he instructed.

I'd never worn a motorcycle helmet, so I held it and studied it a moment. I didn't want to do it wrong. I was pretty sure I'd need to tighten the strap that went under my chin.

Tripp's hand reached out as he took the helmet away from me. I glanced up, afraid I'd taken too long and he'd changed his mind. "Sorry. That was rude. I should've done it for you. You've never ridden before," he said simply, then put it on my head and adjusted the straps.

He was so close I could smell him. He had some wonderful scent that I assumed was cologne, which mixed with the sea breeze. I inhaled deeply as he fixed the helmet.

"There you go. We got that gorgeous head all safe and sound now," he said as he stepped back from me and threw a leg over the bike. "Grab my shoulders and climb on back. Hold on to me as tight as you need."

He had just called my head *gorgeous*. I couldn't think about anything else at the moment. I was too focused on that. Was I asleep? Was this another one of my dreams? If so, it was a really good one. Except we weren't kissing yet. I liked the dreams when we were kissing the best.

I walked over and placed my hands on his shoulders as he instructed, then slung my leg over the seat and sat down behind him. He said to hold on tight, but did he mean to his shoulders? I had seen people on motorcycles enough to know the riders on the back typically wrapped their arms around the drivers, but I didn't know if Tripp wanted me to do that. Before I could think about it any more, he reached back and pulled my arms around his middle.

"Tight, sweetheart. Hold on tight," he repeated, and I did.

Pressing my chest against Tripp's back was amazing. With every breath I took, all I could smell was him. I felt the hard warmth of his back against my chest, and everything tingled. I was thankful it was dark and he couldn't see exactly how much my body was enjoying this.

The Harley came to life underneath us, and we were off. The hold I had on Tripp instantly tightened as he sped toward the main road. My heart was beating so fast I was sure he could feel it. This was exciting. I never did dangerous things. I was responsible. I had to be. My dad wasn't around much, and when he was, he didn't want me there. I was a constant reminder of my mother, who had left him with a kid and run off with another man. He hated her for abandoning him. Not us. Just him. He was selfish, but then, so was my mother. So I did everything I could to prove to him that I wasn't like her.

Aunt Darla would be so disappointed in me right now, but I couldn't help it. This was a once-in-a-lifetime experience. Girls like me didn't get to ride on the back of Tripp's bike. He was untouchable. And tonight he'd seen me. He'd saved me. Again.

I was sure there would never be a man who compared to Tripp. He was the epitome of perfection. And I was just another girl from the trailer park. Someone he wouldn't have noticed if it hadn't been for Aunt Darla. He liked her. He was doing this for her.

As much as I needed to remind myself of this, I didn't want to right now. I just wanted to memorize how good his body felt against mine. The taut muscles in his stomach flexed as he turned onto the street that would lead us toward the club and around the wealthier part of town. I lived the other way. In all the excitement of being driven by Tripp, I forgot to tell him where I lived. My trailer wasn't in Rosemary Beach. There weren't trailers in Rosemary Beach. The average house there cost at least five million dollars. My trailer was thirty minutes north of town.

I could have him take me to the club. Aunt Darla would still be working. She lived closer, because Mr. Kerrington supplied her with an apartment on the property. She would be upset with me when I explained what happened, but I couldn't ask Tripp to take me all the way home. It was too far.

"Just take me to Aunt Darla's office," I told him, leaning close enough to his ear so he could hear me over the wind.

He turned his head slightly to the right, closer to me. "I know where her apartment is. I thought that was where you lived."

I wish. Life would be so much easier if I did. Aunt Darla was the one person I knew loved me unconditionally.

"No, but that's OK. I live too far out. I'll just go to her tonight."

Tripp didn't respond at first, and then he slowed down and pulled into a service station. When he came to a stop, I had a moment of panic, because I didn't know what I was supposed to do with my legs. I didn't want to make his bike fall over. That would be horrible.

Tripp placed both legs on the ground. The sight of him

under the lights from the store sign, his wonderful body straddling his Harley, was just another image I would commit to my memory.

Then he turned to look back at me. "Is Darla going to be upset with you about this?"

I could lie to him, but something about those eyes of his made you want to tell him everything. So I shrugged, keeping my mouth shut.

A smirk appeared on his perfectly shaped lips, and my complete focus went to his mouth. The bottom lip was slightly more plump than the top, but it was so slight a difference that most people wouldn't notice. I was just obsessed with him, and I noticed everything. In some of my daydreams, I had sucked on that bottom lip. It was very suckable.

"Bethy?" His voice broke into my fantasies, and I jerked my gaze back up to meet his. He wasn't smirking anymore. He looked amused.

"Hm?" I replied like an idiot. He'd just caught me staring at his mouth.

"I asked you if you'd rather I take you home. I don't mind the longer drive. You've had a rough night. I don't want you having to face an angry Darla."

She would be angry. I wasn't sure what she was going to be more angry about: me going to Rush Finlay's house party with Jonathon or me riding on the back of Tripp's motorcycle. I had a feeling she was going to be equally mad about both.

"I live thirty minutes away," I explained, dropping my gaze to the oil-stained pavement instead of looking into his eyes. I didn't trust myself not to get lost in another daydream.

"With your parents?" he asked.

"My dad."

He let out a low whistle. "Dad or Darla? Which one is gonna be more pissed?"

I let out a sigh. Dad wouldn't be home tonight. He stayed out most Friday and Saturday nights, since he didn't have to work the next day. "Darla. Dad won't be home tonight."

Tripp didn't respond to that right away, so I studied the ground while I waited for him to make up his mind. Going back to my trailer was the best option for me, but I would feel so bad about Tripp having to spend the gas and time doing that. "You often stay home at night alone?" he asked. The concern in his voice surprised me. I glanced up to look at him, and sure enough, he was frowning.

"Just on weekends," I replied, and his frown deepened.

"That isn't safe." He let out a sigh and shook his head. "I'm gonna take you to Darla. I feel better about that. You shouldn't be staying home alone on weekends."

I was almost seventeen! Why was he acting like I was ten? Did I look like a kid? "I turn seventeen in September. I'm not a child. I've been staying home alone on weekends most of my life." I was a little annoyed with him now. I didn't want Tripp to see me as a kid. I would be a junior this year at school.

A grin tugged at his lips, but he was holding it back. I could see him struggle with it. If he weren't so dang beautiful, I'd climb off his bike and hitchhike home. I'd done that before, too.

"Never said you were a child, Bethy. That wasn't what I was thinking when I said it wasn't safe."

All it took was that one sexy look and hearing his warm,

deep voice to have me at his mercy again, enchanted. I'd go wherever he wanted me to.

"OK," I replied.

He laughed this time, then turned around to start the motorcycle again. "Hold on tight," he reminded me.

Once my arms were wrapped around him, we shot back onto the dark road that led to the club. Tonight I'd be facing Aunt Darla's anger. But it was so worth it.

Tripp

Present day

I sat on my Harley and waited for Bethy to walk out of the clubhouse. Woods had been texting me Bethy's work schedule every two weeks, and I made sure she made it home from work safely every night. It wasn't stalking her, exactly. It was just the only way I could remain sane.

Watching over her was all I had. If I got too close, she flipped. The last time I'd tried to talk to her, she'd started screaming. I hadn't been able to calm her down. I was watching her lose herself slowly. And it was tearing me up.

So I followed her to work every day, and I followed her home every night. Once she was safely in her apartment, I often sat parked across the road and watched her window until it went dark. She never looked at me, even though I wasn't hiding the fact that I was following her. There was no use in hiding it from her.

The last words she'd actually spoken to me—not screamed at me, because there'd been a lot of that—had been eighteen months ago on the beach when we'd lost Jace. My cousin, my

18

best friend, and the love of Bethy's life. He'd drowned saving her life when she'd wandered into the ocean drunk and got caught in a riptide. Losing him had taken a part of my soul. He'd been the little brother I never had. He'd been the good Newark heir. He'd been everything I should have been but wasn't.

And we had loved the same girl. Although he never knew it.

Watching her pull away from life more and more each day was so damn hard. Jace wouldn't have wanted this. He would have hated it. He loved her more than he loved himself. Seeing her like this would have broken his heart.

Bethy swung her long dark hair over her shoulder as she stepped out of the clubhouse. The shorts she wore had once been tight and cupped her perfect round bottom. But just like she'd lost the will to live, she'd also lost weight. Too much.

The need to hold her and help her heal was so fucking strong. But she didn't want me. I hadn't realized how badly she hated me until I'd returned to Rosemary Beach a little more than two years ago. I'd run like hell eight years ago from a life threatening to suffocate me. My father had wanted something for me that I didn't want, and I hadn't been able to see my way out.

I'd been eighteen years old and scared, because in three short months, one sixteen-year-old girl had become my sole concern in life. Bethy had stolen my heart the summer I met her at Rush's party. When I'd been ready to throw away the life I'd been planning for the past year in order to be with her, my father had reminded me of just how much control he had over me.

I wouldn't have been able to keep Bethy if I'd stayed. That

wasn't the life he'd let me have. So I'd run, hoping that when I came back in two years, when she was old enough, I could take her with me. But first, I'd needed to escape.

I watched as Bethy opened the door to her old beat-up Ford Taurus and climbed inside. The stiff way she held herself and the way she kept her focus turned away from me told me she knew I was here. She expected me to be here.

Once she would have broken into the biggest, most beautiful smile in the world and run into my arms. But that was the past. I had broken that. I had broken her, and I hadn't even known.

I started my bike and rumbled out onto the road, giving Bethy enough space as I followed her home. She rarely went anywhere else now. Some days she'd go to Grant and Harlow's to visit with them and their baby girl. Other days she would go to Blaire and Rush's. But other than those rare times, she just went home.

Her home was another thing that was eating me alive. I hated it. I hated leaving her at night to sleep in an apartment fifteen miles outside of town with questionable neighbors. She'd had a nice condo on the club's property, completely paid for, but after Jace's death, she moved out. Blaire said she needed to get away from the memories, that the beach was too painful for her.

But God, I hated it. Bethy deserved more than this life. The young girl with those big, soft brown eyes, so trusting and innocent, haunted me. Because of me, that girl was gone. I'd destroyed that trust and innocence.

Bethy's car turned into the service station just inside the town limits. She didn't need to get gasoline. I knew that because I knew the days she needed to fill up. She'd done so two days ago. She still had several more days before she needed more. I parked across the road and watched her.

I watched her park her car and get out. She gripped the door as she turned and glared in my direction before she slammed the door. At least she looked at me this time. I expected her to go back to ignoring me and go inside, but she didn't.

She kept her angry gaze locked on me as she stalked across the parking lot and headed my way. *Oh, shit.* She was pissed, and there was no one around to calm her the hell down when she went off on me. Maybe this was a good thing. The last time she went off on me, Grant and Woods had held her back and taken her home. Whenever I spoke, she'd just scream louder. Hearing my voice was enough to infuriate her.

I hadn't understood the contempt she'd hidden from Jace and only shown me when no one was looking . . . until that day on the beach. The memory of her words sliced through me, and I winced. That was always going to fucking haunt me. I'd never get over it.

I climbed off my bike and waited for whatever she planned on throwing at me. She was acknowledging my existence. I would take what I could get.

She stopped in front of me and put her hands on her hips. Even with the weight loss, Bethy still had hips. They were thinner, but they were there. She had fantastic hips. "Stop following me," she demanded, fury flashing in her eyes. "I don't need you stalking my ass like a psycho!"

I had to tread carefully with her. I wanted her to talk to me; I didn't want to piss her off. "I'm just making sure you're safe," I replied in the softest tone I could muster.

Bethy let out a frustrated growl. "Don't! I don't need you making sure I'm safe. It doesn't matter if I'm safe. I haven't been your concern in a very long time." She was trying to control herself. She wanted to hit me. Scream at me. She wanted to blame someone else for Jace's death, and I was the easiest person to hate.

"It matters to me that you're safe," I said simply.

She closed her eyes and took a deep breath. Her hands were clenched tightly in fists as they rested on her hips. "I don't like seeing you. I don't like you watching me. I want to be left alone. I'm going to get a restraining order against you, Tripp, I swear to God," she threatened.

We both knew I had done nothing to her and she wouldn't be able to get a restraining order. But telling her that would only upset her. "I know you hate me. For a long time, I didn't know why. But I do now. Hell, Bethy, I hate myself," I admitted. "That doesn't mean I don't care about you. I'm worried about you, and if you don't want me near you, I get it. But I'm going to keep you as safe as I can. I'm sorry if that upsets you."

Bethy let out a hysterical laugh that wasn't a laugh at all. I loved Bethy's laugh. The one when she was happy. Hearing her laugh and watching her smile had once owned me. I'd do anything for it. Now it was nothing more than a hollow, hard sound that only added to the pain between us.

"Why did you come back? I was fine. Jace and I were great. I was happy, Tripp. I was so damn happy." Her voice cracked, and I wanted to reach for her. The hard, angry shell she'd surrounded herself with was cracking. "Seeing you ruined it. Everything! It ruined everything. Then . . . you . . ." she let out a scream and pressed her hands over her eyes. "I tried to make us all work. I tried to like you. I tried to accept that Jace loved you, and I wanted to forget the past. I wanted to forget that summer. I had Jace. Why did you have to remind me? Why did you have to . . ." She swallowed hard. "I was happy. I had thought Jace was my one. Then you came back and screwed it all up. Why?" Her voice was so broken. Tears filled her eyes as she glared at me.

I had come back with the excuse of checking on my friend Della Sloane. I'd met her in Dallas at a restaurant where she was a waitress and I was a bartender. I had sent her here to get a job at the club and live in my condo after she'd slept with our boss, who she hadn't known was married at the time. I hadn't lived in the condo since that summer I met Bethy, when my grandfather gave it to me as a graduation present. I had sent Della to the one place I knew she'd be safe. I had been right. She was now engaged to Woods Kerrington and was blissfully happy.

At the time, I told myself I'd come home because I'd heard Jace's voice on the phone and had missed home. I'd known Jace was with Bethy, and as hard as that was to accept, he was the better man. He was good for her.

Looking back now, I could admit I came home for her. I wanted to see Bethy. I wanted to see if time and distance had truly ended what we once had.

They hadn't.

"I wanted to come home," I said, unable to tell her the full truth.

Bethy's shoulders sagged, and she crossed her arms over her stomach protectively. "We were happy. You ruined it."

She didn't have to explain. I understood. When I had

walked up to Jace's door and Bethy had answered it, it was as if all those years had vanished. The girl who had shown me that love really was worth fighting for had stood there, older but more beautiful than I'd remembered. She was my girl. And she was wearing my cousin's T-shirt, looking like she'd just crawled out of his bed.

We hadn't spoken. We'd just stood there and looked at each other. For a moment, I'd almost expected her to jump into my arms, but then Jace had walked up behind her and wrapped his arms around her waist, grinning up at me like the happiest man on earth.

The world had fallen out from under me at that moment. Although I had known I'd lost her, it didn't hit home until then. All these years, I'd lived with a guarded heart. I never got close to a girl. My heart had been claimed years ago. Not once had I been tempted to give it to anyone else.

"I'm sorry," I said finally. And I *was* sorry. I was sorry I had come home. Because she was right. It had ruined everything she had built. I hadn't been able to stop eating her up with my eyes, had been unable to get my fill of her. When Jace wasn't around, I'd watched her hungrily, like my last breath depended on it. We never spoke, but words weren't needed. I'd said enough with my eyes.

"You will always remind me of what I lost. Twice. I only lose with you, Tripp. You leave destruction in your wake. I can't handle losing anything more."

More than once since Jace had drowned, I wished to God it had been me. If I had been there that night, I would have saved his life. I wouldn't have let him drown saving Bethy. I'd have beaten him to those waves. It would have been me who drowned that night. And all would have been right with the world.

Hearing Bethy tell me what I already knew, and what I already dealt with every day when I opened my eyes, made it impossible to breathe. I wasn't worth the air I breathed. Knowing that the woman I'd love until the day I died believed the same thing made life seem pointless.

Which was why I would continue to keep her safe. I had to make this life mean something. This life I didn't deserve. Keeping Bethy safe didn't just mean something, it meant everything.

She didn't wait for me to respond. She turned and walked back across the street, then climbed into her car. I waited until she was on the road and headed home before I pulled out onto the road and followed her.

Bethy

I stood behind my curtains and stared across the street at Tripp. He was sitting on his bike with his eyes fixed on my window. Normally, he left when I turned out the light at night. Once he was gone, I'd turn it back on. Tonight he wasn't leaving. I had turned off the light an hour ago, and he was still sitting there, watching my window.

I had been numb for so long that ignoring him hadn't been difficult. But lately, it was getting to me. The numbness I had embraced was slowly fading away, and long-buried emotions were finding their way to the surface, past my shield.

There had been a time when I was angry at the world, but I thought I'd moved on from that part of the mourning process. I had cried out all my tears. When the numbness came, I held it close. I wanted that. I needed it in order to continue living. The guilt and pain were tearing me apart.

Woods hadn't been able to look at me because of the role I had played in Jace's death, and I'd held on to that. He hated me still. He knew it was my fault. I clung to that. I needed to be hated. I didn't need pity. I didn't deserve pity. I should be hated. I wanted to be hated. Woods gave me that.

Everyone else worried about me. I didn't want them to

worry about me. They all saw what had happened. They all should hate me. But they didn't. I stayed away from them, because the pity was too much. It wasn't me they should worry about. I wasn't worth their worry. I wasn't worth their sympathy.

Then there was Tripp. As much as I wanted him to, he wouldn't leave. He wouldn't go away.

He no longer tried to speak to me. He had stopped that a long time ago. But he was always there in my damn rearview mirror, following me. Standing off in the shadows, watching me like some insane protector. I didn't need protection. Especially not his.

I pulled my wrap tighter around me and sat down on my sofa in the dark. This was my only refuge. My apartment. A place Jace had never been before. There were no memories of happier times here. Except that Tripp invaded this world each night by sitting out there, watching me.

After he'd ruined me, I'd used my body to find happiness. I'd told myself I was looking for someone else, but I'd really been trying to wash him from my memories. So I'd partied. And I'd slept with guys. I'd become someone completely different from the girl he'd left behind.

Each time I closed my eyes and gave my body to another guy, I hoped I would forget Tripp.

But I never did.

He was always there in the back of my mind. The sweet, gentle way he'd held me our first time, even as he reminded me that there was more out there. Then I would remember how much it hurt to lose that.

Jace had come along, and I'd wanted him simply because he looked so much like Tripp. He reminded me of him, too.

He wasn't like the others. At first, he used me for sex, but he kept coming back. He made me smile, and he said sweet things.

When I had decided to stand up for myself and stop giving my body away to whatever wealthy hot guy hit on me, Jace had made a move, and just like Cinderella, I'd finally found love with my prince.

I had been so scared to love Jace, but he'd made it hard not to. I'd been older than when I'd met Tripp, and I'd told myself that it had been different with him because that had been a young love. I'd fallen deeper and more intensely because I'd been young. I had lived in a fairy tale.

What I'd had with Jace was real. I'd held on to that, and for a brief time, I'd been happy. Then Tripp had come back to Rosemary Beach, and one look at him, and my heart had slammed against my chest. All that intensity I had told myself was a young girl's fascination had swamped me, overwhelming me immediately. I hated that he brought that out in me.

I hated what he'd done to me.

I hated him.

But I faked it because Jace loved him. And Jace could never know what had happened between Tripp and me.

The sound of Tripp's motorcycle roaring to life made me breathe a sigh of relief. He was finally leaving. I hated the dark. I hadn't eaten all day, and I needed to fix myself something before I went to bed.

Sitting in the silence, I waited ten minutes before standing up and turning on the lights. Tripp was gone for the night. I wouldn't have to see him again until the morning, when he'd return while I was getting ready for work.

Tonight I had acknowledged him. I had spoken to him. I had wanted to spew all the hate and pain I had inside me at him. I knew he would take it—I knew he wouldn't look at me with sympathy. And I had been right. He was Tripp. Calm, solid Tripp.

The words I'd said tonight had been harsh and cruel. Guilt settled inside me. He didn't deserve that, but I had said them anyway. His flinching at my words had been the only sign that they affected him. Jace would hate who I had become. But I couldn't stop myself.

The numbness was finally gone. Life was sinking in. Reality was here. I had to move on.

Everything had changed when Harlow gave birth. Harlow was my friend and Grant's fiancée. They'd accidentally gotten pregnant, even though Harlow had a heart condition that made pregnancy risky, and for a little while after the birth, we weren't sure she was going to make it. We'd been camped out in the hospital lobby when Woods had walked up to me. He'd told me it wasn't my fault that Jace was gone. He'd been wrong for holding it against me; he just hadn't been able to accept that Jace was gone. He was still angry, but he wanted me to be happy again and he knew Jace would want that, too. Then he'd hugged me.

The numbness had begun to fade in that moment, and I'd almost begged him to hate me. I needed his hate. But the sincerity in his eyes as he'd squeezed my shoulders and told me to find happiness again had rendered me mute. Della had broken down in a fit of tears and come up to me and hugged me after watching Woods forgive me. It had all been too much.

Since that day, everything was changing. My secure world

of nothingness was crumbling. And Tripp was still there, following me.

I was scared of depending on him, because this would end, too. He would leave. And I'd be left with one more thing to move on from. He needed to leave now. I knew from experience that he would only find ways to destroy me. I couldn't live again if I had to guard myself from Tripp.

Tripp

Eight years ago

"What the hell is going on down at the beach?" I muttered as we pulled up to the condo my grandfather had given me as a graduation present. My parents hadn't been happy about it, but my mother's father had informed them that I needed my own space apart from them. This was his gift to me. I'd moved out the next day. Having the freedom of my own place allowed me to get the hell out of my parents' clutches. It offered a taste of what I could have.

"Looks like a bonfire," Woods said, stating the obvious.

"And we weren't invited?" Jace asked.

"It's not our crowd. We're real close to the town limits. That part of the beach isn't Rosemary Beach. My guess is they're from Destin. Locals, maybe," Woods explained.

We got out of Woods's truck, and I grinned back at the other two. I was leaving soon, and I wanted to spend as much time as I could with Jace and his friends before I left. I didn't know when I'd be home again. I had my own friends, too, but I could visit them when I was on the road. None of them spent summers here. I always did, because I was close to the guys from boarding school. The one year I'd spent there with Jace, Woods, and Thad had been epic. The shit we got away with because of Woods's daddy's influence . . . Whenever Rush Finlay came to visit Grant, we really got to have some fun. No one wanted to piss off a rock god's son.

"Let's go find some trouble," I suggested, and Woods laughed as Jace whooped and jumped down out of the truck.

"I bet there're hotties in bikinis lookin' for a good time in that crowd," Thad piped up as he pulled his long blond hair back into a ponytail.

"That's what I'm thinking. I haven't gotten any since I broke up with London," I admitted.

"Damn, she's fucking hot. I haven't figured out why you stopped tapping that ass," Thad said.

"She's crazy," Woods told him. He knew the stories. He'd heard them from Jace.

I nodded my head in agreement.

"I'm going to go grab that six-pack out of the fridge," Jace said.

"I gotta use some mouthwash," Woods said, following him up to my condo.

"I'll meet y'all down there," I told them. Thad followed the other two; I figured he was going after the mouthwash, too. They were all sixteen, and I doubted any of them would be getting any tonight, but I didn't break it to them. This crowd was probably my age or older.

I stepped into the firelight and looked around. The bikinis were gonna make Thad really happy. Smiling, I went over to stand on the outskirts of the party to watch from the shadows for a bit before seeing if this was anything I wanted to walk into.

A large piece of driftwood lay just up to the right, hidden in the shadows, and I could make out the silhouette of someone occupying it. I knew that piece of driftwood. I came out here often at night to sit and watch the waves.

Curious, I walked over to it. As I approached, the occupant of my seat turned to look up at me. The moonlight illuminated her perfectly, and I recognized the sweet face and big brown eyes watching me. Bethy.

I hadn't seen her again since I took her to her aunt Darla's last weekend, yet I'd heard she kept finding the parties in town. At least this time, she was alone and not fighting off a jerk.

"You always find the good parties?" I asked as I sat down beside her.

She didn't respond at first, and I wondered if she remembered me. "Tripp," I reminded her. "I gave you a ride from Rush's party last weekend."

She smiled and ducked her head. "I know who you are," she said softly, but that husky tone in her voice gave me a little shiver. I had to remember this girl was too young for me.

"Good. Then I'm not that forgettable," I joked.

She laughed and glanced back up at me. "I knew who you were last weekend."

Interesting. But then, she'd grown up at the club. I'd seen her many times myself. "So, whose party is this?" I asked, looking out at the crowd before turning my gaze back to her.

She sighed. "People from school. Seniors, mostly. My friend got an invite from a senior guy she has a thing for. She didn't want to come alone. So here I am."

And she was sitting all alone in the dark. Not exactly safe.

"Where's your friend now?" I asked.

"There, in that American flag bikini with that guy who has his hand down her bottoms," she said, pointing to the couple openly making out in front of everyone. "She doesn't always make smart choices," Bethy said with a frown as she looked away from her friend and back down at her hands clasped in her lap.

She was also wearing a swimsuit, but she had a cover-up on. I could see the pink straps tied behind her neck. All she was showing off was her legs. Her really long legs.

"Why are you here?" she asked, looking back up at me.

I nodded my head back to the condos to the left of us. "I live there."

She frowned. "I thought your parents' place was on the other side of Rosemary Beach."

She knew where my parents' summer house was? That was surprising. I wondered what else she knew about me. "I moved out after graduation," I explained.

She sighed wistfully. "That must be nice."

She had no idea. But then, she didn't know what I was about to run from. She didn't have people trying to make life decisions for her. That was my hell to face.

Hoots and whistles stopped me from saying anything more. I glanced out at the crowd to see that Bethy's friend was topless, and the guy she was with was sucking on her tits right there in front of everyone. The girl's head was thrown back as she held his head to her chest.

"Oh, God," Bethy said beside me.

"Your friend is a bit of an exhibitionist," I said, looking

away from the action in front of me to Bethy, who was watching, horrified.

"She's lost her mind. I don't know what's gotten into her lately," Bethy said, covering her eyes. "I do *not* want to see that."

Laughing, I reached over and took her hands from her face. "Take a walk with me. Maybe they'll be done with this when we get back. We can miss the actual public sex."

Bethy sighed and slipped her hand into mine, then nodded. "OK. Yeah. Because at this rate, they're probably going to do it."

Woods, Thad, and Jace needed to hurry and get down here for the show. It was probably the only action they were getting tonight.

We headed away from the condo and further into the darkness. I kept Bethy's hand in mine, because it felt good. As long as she was good with it, I was keeping it there.

"How old is your friend?" I asked her.

"She turned seventeen last week. Her parents are getting divorced, and she's taking it hard. Her mom walked into her room a month ago and caught her giving a guy head. It was bad. She's lost her mind. But her parents aren't doing much to stop her."

"Might not be smart to follow her to parties. Can't be safe for you. Guys might think you're open to that stuff, too," I said. I didn't like the idea of any guy forcing himself on Bethy. She was so damn sweet, with a body that was way too mature for her. I did my best not to ogle her. It was easier to think of her as the sixteen-year-old girl she was if I wasn't looking at her very developed assets.

"If this is what she intends to do at these parties, I won't be coming with her anymore. I don't want to watch her do this. Besides, I start working at the club next week. I won't have time to party with her. I'm saving up to get my own place as soon as I graduate."

She would be working at the club? I liked that. More than I should. "Really? What will you be doing?"

"The only job Mr. Kerrington will allow Aunt Darla to hire me for is the lifeguard position at the pool."

So she'd be in one of those red swimsuits all day. Even more appealing. I never visited the pool at the club, but I just might start. "I'm sure you'll wear the uniform well," I said, unable not to say it. I was flirting, but damn, it was hard not to.

She stopped walking a moment and glanced up at me with those big eyes. I had surprised her. Which made her even more damn appealing. She was actually surprised that I thought she'd look good in a swimsuit.

"What?" I asked, grinning.

"I have to wear a swimsuit," she said slowly, like I hadn't realized what her uniform would be.

I nodded. "Yeah."

She glanced down at herself like she was checking to see if I saw the same thing she did. "You can see that I'm overweight, right?" she finally said, looking back up at me.

What? Was she joking? "Are you kidding?" I asked.

She shook her head slowly as she watched me like she was waiting for me to notice something. Did the girl really not know her body was incredible? Or was she fishing for a compliment? She didn't have the teasing, flirty smile most girls had when they wanted you to compliment them. She looked pretty damn serious.

"You're not overweight," I said, letting my gaze drop back to her swimsuit cover-up.

"You must not have seen me clearly last weekend. My . . . I have large body parts," she said, and started walking again. This time, she wasn't holding my hand. She looked like she was trying to get away from me.

I took two steps toward her, grabbed her hand, and stopped her. "Bethy, we are so not done with this conversation. Come here," I said as she reluctantly glanced back at me.

"Please, let's drop this," she said.

I shook my head. "Not a chance."

She tensed and turned back around to look at me. "I'm sorry I said anything. Let's talk about something else."

"Take off your cover-up," I told her. I might not make a move on her, but I was damn well going to show her how hot her body was. She needed to be aware of it so that she'd protect herself.

Her eyes went wide, and this time she shook her head.

"Please, Bethy. For me," I said, using all the skills I had perfected to charm females.

She faltered and then let out a heavy sigh before taking the hem of her cover-up and pulling it up over her head. She didn't let it drop to the sand but held it in her hand tightly by her side as she closed her eyes, unable to look at me.

I was glad for that moment to pull myself together. I had been able to tell that her body was smoking under her clothes, but seeing it in a bikini was something else. Her tits were about to tumble out of that small top, and her hips . . . damn, her hips were perfect. She had a tiny waist, but the way her hips flared told me her backside was going to be fucking amazing. Then there were those legs.

"Told you," she said quietly.

My eyes snapped back up to her face as she looked at me with an unsure, nervous, forced smile. She started to lift her cover-up to put it back on, but I reached for her arm to stop her. "No," I said. I wasn't done looking. I might never be done looking.

"This is embarrassing," she said in a whisper.

I swallowed hard. Fuck, I was gonna be getting off to this image for months. *Too young, Tripp. Too young. She's too young.* "Turn around," I said.

She shook her head. "No, I can't. That's worse."

Holy hell, she was blind. "Right now, I'm having to remind myself that you're too young. I'm eighteen, and that makes you illegal. But this view makes it hard to care. I don't know who told you that you're overweight, but sweetheart, you're fucking perfect."

Bethy's breathing picked up, and her chest rose and fell. I really wanted to tug that top down and get my hands and eyes full of her tits. "Really?" she asked.

I nodded. "Will you please turn around now?" I asked, knowing this was going to fuck me up. If the view got any better, I was a goner. That sweet smile and beautiful face didn't need to come with this package. It was too much.

She slowly turned, and her round, firm ass was barely covered up by the bottom she was wearing. The suit wasn't meant for a girl with a body like this. I was so fucking thankful she had that cover-up on. If the guys at that party had gotten a look at her, they'd have swarmed like ravenous vultures.

"Fuck," I muttered, unable not to comment.

She quickly spun back around, and her bottom lip was caught between her teeth. She was worried again. "I know it's big," she said, almost apologetically.

I had to draw a line with her in my head. Because I was about to make a huge mistake. I would be leaving soon, and I couldn't touch her. Even if I wanted to, real damn bad. Bethy was too sweet. Too innocent. I wasn't someone who should get to touch her. "No. It's not too big. It's sexy, Bethy. Your whole body is sexy as hell. You make guys think things and want things. You need to be aware of that. Wearing a swimsuit like that can push a guy over the edge. You've got a body guys fantasize over. I won't be able to get it out of my head for a very long time. So this shit about you being overweight is insane. Don't ever think you are less than gorgeous. And protect that. Now, put that cover-up back on. Please," I said.

Bethy didn't move right away, and I soaked in the last view I was going to get of her body. When she pulled the cover-up back over her head, I took a deep breath again. "Thank you," she said finally.

"For what?" I asked.

"For making me feel beautiful."

Bethy

One week working in the sun, and my tan was darker than it had ever been. I had been dreading wearing a swimsuit and sitting on a lifeguard stand where people could see me. But thanks to Tripp, this week hadn't been the awful experience I thought it would be. I didn't feel fat. I felt like I looked nice. The lifeguard suit covered up a lot more than the one Meredith had let me borrow for the party.

I rarely saw people my age at the pool, so it wasn't that big a deal anyway. It was mostly young mothers and their kids. Some girls my age and older came to lie out, but most of them did that at the beach, not the pool. My biggest problem this week had been Chad. He was one of the lifeguards and had taken an interest in me. Which was proving to be annoying. I wasn't interested back, but he wasn't getting the hint.

I coated my face with some more sunblock and put my sunglasses back on before climbing down the ladder to switch spots with Fern, another lifeguard, who had been working the shallow end. Everyone wanted one of the stands with the umbrellas. Working the shallow end was exhausting, but I was ready to get wet and cool off, so I didn't mind the switch.

"Hottie alert. Tripp Newark just walked in," Fern whispered as she walked over to me, grinning.

I quickly searched for him and found him standing near the entrance, already stopped by one of the servers who catered to the pool area. I felt a twinge of jealousy as he bent his head and whispered in her ear. The server giggled, and he smirked before walking toward the pool. I watched as his eyes went to the lifeguard stand and scanned the crowd until they met mine.

The silly smile on my face was there before I could stop it. Tripp grinned, and he did a slow scan of me in the swimsuit before he met my eyes again. He nodded with an appreciative gleam in his eyes that made butterflies in my stomach take flight.

"Ohmygod, he's looking at you," Fern said in an awed tone.

"He's a friend," I explained before she embarrassed me. I didn't want Tripp to think that he had to come speak to me or that I expected it.

I gave him one last smile before heading to the shallow end of the pool. He had a towel in his hand, but I wasn't going to assume he was here to hang out at the pool. He might just have been passing through.

I also had to make sure no kid drowned on my watch. Lusting over Tripp wasn't a good idea any way you looked at it.

I walked into the pool and cooled off before sitting down on the edge, where the lifeguard for the section was supposed to stay. I didn't give in and look for Tripp. It took all my self-control, but I managed it for at least ten minutes.

When the lack of action in the pool became too much, I glanced casually over toward the lounge chairs lined up under umbrellas and found Tripp easily enough. He was talking to the server who had flirted with him when he got here. She was older. I would guess she was even a year or two older than Tripp. He seemed to enjoy her attention, and that was too painful to watch. I jerked my gaze off him and back to the kids in the pool.

"It's your break," Chad's familiar voice said as he sat down beside me. "I'm here to rescue you."

I glanced at him and forced a smile. I wasn't sure I liked him much. He had made several comments about my body that embarrassed me. "Thanks," I said, standing up.

"That's a nice view," he said as I turned my back to him. I cringed at the idea of him staring at my bottom.

I didn't respond or react. It was best just to ignore Chad's comments. I headed for the break room where I had left my lunch box this morning. I had been here for three hours, but I was starving.

When I walked around the corner into the staff-only section, I heard footsteps behind me. Glancing back, I saw Tripp and stopped short. What was he doing?

"Hey," he said.

"Hey," I replied, but it sounded like I was asking a question. Which I kind of was.

"You on break?" he asked.

I nodded, still not sure why he had followed me.

"You have something to put on over your suit?"

I nodded again.

This time, he grinned. "Put it on, and let's go eat."

Let's go eat. He wanted to eat. With me. "OK," I said obediently. Like I was going to say no to this.

"I've already got a pizza waiting for us and a reserved room. I handled that when I got here."

Oh, wow. OK. I reached into the bag on my shoulder and pulled out my cover-up and put it on. "Ready," I said, and he held out his hand.

"Come on. I'm starving. I know you have to be."

Again, I just nodded. I was so confused.

Tripp led me to the back entrance of the pool café and to a back room reserved for private parties. One table was set with a pizza and two drinks waiting for us.

"I just got regular Coke. If you want something else, just let me know, and I'll have Crystal get it. She's the one who set this up for me."

"Coke is good," I replied, stupidly.

"Did I take you away from lunch plans?" he asked, looking concerned.

I was acting like an idiot. I needed to snap out of this. I shook my head. "No. I was going to eat in the break room. I packed a lunch, but it's just a turkey sandwich and an apple. This is so much better."

Tripp grinned again and pulled out a chair for me. "Good."

I sat down, and he took the chair across from me. "How's the job going?" he asked, reaching for a piece of pizza and putting it on my plate.

I was beginning to think I may have passed out from heat stroke and this was some crazy dream I'd worked up. "I, uh, it's OK. I mean, I like it."

Tripp got a piece of pizza and put it on his plate. "I was right about the suit. You make it look good."

I blushed and ducked my head to hide my stupid reaction.

"Been to any wild parties this week?" he asked in a teasing tone.

I laughed and shook my head. "No. It's all work and no play," I told him, and picked up the pizza. It smelled delicious, and my stomach was now growling.

"I left off the olives. I love olives, but I wasn't sure you liked them," he said as he watched me take a bite. I wouldn't admit it, but I would have eaten anything he put on this pizza. Just because he got it for me. No guy had ever bought me food before.

"I like olives," I said after I swallowed.

He nodded. "Noted. Next time, I can have my olives."

Next time. OK. There was going to be a next time that he bought me pizza.

"Do you work weekends?" Tripp asked me.

"No. I'm only working Monday through Friday this summer."

Tripp took a drink and studied me a moment. Having his complete attention made me nervous. "I've got to drive over to New Orleans on Saturday to pick something up. Want to take a ride?"

I had to be suffering from heat stroke. There was no other explanation. "Sure. Sounds fun," I replied. If I was going to hallucinate, I might as well enjoy myself.

Tripp

Present day

I had parked my bike and was leaning against it with my arms crossed over my chest, waiting. Bethy still had ten more minutes before her shift was over, but I had gotten out of a board meeting with Woods an hour ago, and there was no point leaving and coming back so soon.

Heels clicked on the pavement, and I turned to see Della walking toward me. Her normally happy smile was gone, and a worried frown replaced it. She was getting married in a couple of weeks. I had the invitation on my kitchen counter. I still hadn't bought them a gift.

"You waiting on Bethy?" she asked as she stopped in front of me.

I nodded. She knew I did this on the days Bethy worked.

"She still refusing to talk to you?"

I nodded again. I didn't want to talk about last week and everything Bethy had said. Some things were too painful to verbalize.

"I hate seeing you like this. I wish you'd explain what's

going on. No one understands why Bethy hates you so much and why you follow her daily to make sure she's OK. It's a devotion that I've only seen from men who are in love, but how can you be in love with Bethy? You hardly know her. You weren't here long enough to get to know her, and she was Jace's girlfriend. Something isn't adding up, Tripp. You're my friend. When I needed someone, you were there for me every time. I love you, and I hate seeing you do this to yourself. Maybe you need to get away again and put some distance between you and Rosemary Beach."

I once hoped I could feel something more for Della, but her heart had been with Woods Kerrington before I even met her. I just hadn't known it. Didn't matter, though. We were always meant to be friends.

"I can't leave her" was all I said. Della deserved to know more. She had confided in me when she had no one else to talk to, and I knew she'd be there for me in the same way. We had been close. But this . . . this was more than I could tell anyone. It was a story I wasn't ready to share.

Della sighed and reached out to squeeze my arm. "I want someone to help her. I do. We all do. But Tripp, why you?"

I tore my eyes away from the door to glance down at Della. "Because I've loved her since I was eighteen years old. That's all I can tell you. And please, don't repeat that to anyone." Admitting that to someone other than myself was freeing in a way.

Della's eyes went wide in shock, and she was speechless. She knew more than anyone else now. "Oh, wow," she whispered. "Did . . . OK. Um . . . wow," she stuttered, unsure how to respond.

It was our secret, and now I had told someone. The time I had with Bethy wasn't something I wanted to shove under a rug or keep hidden anymore. I was tired of hiding the truth. If Jace had lived, I'd have taken the secret to my grave. But he was gone. And I was going to be here for the day Bethy was ready to talk to me.

The door opened, and Bethy stepped out. She swung her gaze over to me, and for a brief moment, we stood there staring at each other. She was acknowledging me. Why?

"I gotta go," I told Della, throwing a leg over my bike and watching as Bethy climbed into her car.

"Did she . . . did she cheat on Jace with you?" Della asked as if she was afraid of the answer.

"No. She loved Jace," I replied, and the relief was obvious as Della let out a breath. I cranked up the bike and nodded a good-bye before following Bethy's car out of the parking lot.

☒

I stood on my balcony, watching the waves crash against the shore, unable to sleep. It was how I spent most of my evenings. I hadn't wanted to leave Bethy's tonight. I'd watched her shadow in the darkness as she watched me from her window. As long as I could see her watching me, I wasn't leaving her. But once she finally walked away, I knew it was time to leave. She wanted me to leave.

A knock on my door brought me out of my thoughts. I walked back through the balcony's French doors, wondering who it was. No one came over this late. The hope that it was Bethy was brief and fleeting. When I opened the front door and saw Woods standing there, I knew Della hadn't been able to keep what I'd said to herself. I knew deep down when I admitted it to her that she'd tell one person. The one person she told everything to. I accepted that. I stepped back and waved him inside.

Woods didn't speak as he stepped into the condo and walked into the living area.

"She told you what I said." I decided to get to the point of this visit.

"She's asleep and has no idea I'm here. But yes, she told me because she's worried about you. And worried about Bethy. I'm here because I'm confused as hell. I've tried every fucking scenario in my head I could think of, and nothing makes sense. Eighteen? You left town when you were eighteen. Bethy would have been, what, sixteen?"

I walked over to the open doors and stared outside, unable to look at him. Admitting this to Della was one thing, but telling Woods, Jace's best friend, was another. I already had Bethy's hatred to deal with. I didn't want Woods's, too. Even if I deserved it. "The summer before I left," I reminded him. "You were around. And you know how I was missing a lot. No one knew where and with who."

Woods blew out a breath and muttered a curse. "That was Bethy?"

He remembered. I'd been so caught up in her, and I'd gotten into the habit of giving excuses whenever they wanted to hang out. "Yeah," I said simply.

"Holy fuck. I can't believe that was Bethy."

"I was coming back for her when I could. But she was too young, and I'd have ended up in jail if we'd been caught. She was my secret. I almost didn't leave because of her. But then my dad found out and made it very clear that my time in Rosemary Beach was over. I'd spend the school year at Yale and my summers in Manhattan at the firm. If I stayed, I'd lose her. If I ran, then I had a chance of coming back for her."

Woods didn't respond at first.

This was a secret I'd carried for a long time. It was one that had changed everything for me. I understood that. I was ready to accept it. If everyone hated me, then I'd deal with that, too. All that mattered now was that I watched over Bethy. She was all I had left.

"Jace was going to ask her to marry him," Woods said finally.

"I know. He was the better man. He was going to give her the life she deserved, and I wanted that for her. I wanted her happy. I wanted her to have a life she was meant for. She loved him. That's what mattered. I was her past. A past she hates now."

Woods walked over to stand beside me. "He never knew?"

I shook my head. "No. There was no reason to tell him. Bethy was his. I'd lost her long ago."

"But you love her."

"More than my next breath," I replied.

"Shit," Woods muttered.

I wouldn't tell him any more. Her reasons for hating me were her secrets to share. Not mine.

"She hates you for leaving?" he asked.

She hated me for destroying everything. She hated me for not being there when she needed me. "I remind her of all she lost with Jace. She needs to hate someone, so she hates me. And I'll accept that. I'll be whatever she needs me to be."

Woods stood there beside me and didn't ask anything else. But he didn't blame me. He didn't get angry at me. He just stood there with me.

Bethy

Harlow and Grant's wedding had been easy to celebrate because of the simple fact that Harlow was alive, standing at the
altar with their miracle baby. I had gone to the wedding and
cried happy tears because Grant had his wife and child. He
hadn't lost them after all.

Now, three months later, not only did I have to attend another wedding, but I had to be in it. I couldn't just show up for
a couple of hours and pretend to smile. We would be spending
four days on a private island that Woods had rented out for the
wedding. He had wanted something intimate where he didn't
feel like he had to invite every member of the country club. So
he had found this island near the Florida Keys that could be
rented for weddings and other special events. Only close family and friends had been invited, all expenses paid.

Then there was the fact that Tripp was also in the wedding
party. I had to be around him in a social setting in front of my
friends for four long days. Although I was happy for Della and
Woods, being around Tripp wasn't going to be easy.

Della had told me that Thad would be my escort at the
wedding. After my drunken fit at the club a while ago, when
I'd screamed at Tripp, everyone knew something was wrong

between us, but they couldn't figure out what. They just assumed I was losing my mind. Della wasn't going to take the chance of assigning Tripp as my escort, even though that would have made the most sense before my meltdown, Tripp being Jace's cousin and all.

I stood at the private airport outside of Rosemary Beach. Dean Finlay had offered Slacker Demon's private jet to take the wedding party to the island. Woods and Della had sent plane tickets to the rest of the guests. Except, of course, for the members of Slacker Demon who were also invited. The plane would be taking them to the island later in the week.

Della was standing at the bottom of the stairs leading up to the plane, talking happily to Blaire. These were my friends. I loved them. Being with them should not be hard. Taking a deep breath, I reached for the handle of my rolling suitcase and headed for the plane.

Della's gaze moved to me, and her smile grew. She was so happy. Della had overcome so much. I remembered the girl who had come to Rosemary Beach—sheltered and haunted by her past. Della didn't even resemble that girl anymore. She wasn't a victim. She was a survivor.

"We're all here now," Della said, and stepped forward to hug me. "I'm so glad you're coming. Thank you," she whispered in my ear as she held me firmly before letting go.

"I wouldn't miss this for the world," I told her.

"I'll take that, miss," a man said, holding out his hand for my suitcase.

I handed my luggage over to the crew and then looked at Blaire. "Hey, you," I said, smiling. Blaire was my best friend. Because of her, I'd had Jace. She'd shown me that making myself worthy of love was the way to get the guy I wanted. In many ways, Blaire had helped me find a part of the girl I once was before Tripp. Not entirely, but some of the old me had come back because of Blaire.

Once I had been like Blaire. Strong, confident, independent. But like everything else in life, Tripp took that from me.

"You good?" she asked, studying my face. Only Blaire had the balls to ask me if I was OK. Everyone else had stopped asking, afraid of my reaction. I wanted to tell her that the numbness was gone. But it had been replaced by the feelings I'd been holding back. I had to deal with it all.

But not now. This was Della and Woods's special weekend. I wouldn't ruin it with my sadness. "I'm doing good. I was going to come by last week, but I had to work overtime for several days."

Blaire cocked an eyebrow at me. "Tell that to Nate. He's been asking for 'An Betty' the last few days. He's used to seeing you at least once a week, you know."

That little boy was one of the lights of my life. I loved that kid. I had been so afraid that I wouldn't be able to go near him when he was born. I feared that seeing Blaire and Rush with their baby would be too much for me. I would feel the regret and pain when I looked at him. But it didn't happen. Nate won my heart with his sweet baby smile. He was a charmer from day one. "He'll be here this weekend?" I asked, glancing up at the side of the plane, feeling guilty for not visiting him now.

"He's coming tomorrow night with Dean. His grandfather wanted to keep him at the house and give us one night alone on the island."

I shook my head. The idea that Dean Finlay, the rock god, was taking care of a baby was just funny. But he loved that kid.

"All right, ladies, move the gossip inside. It's time we head south," Woods said as he stood at the top of the stairs. His eyes were locked on Della's. I had known Woods since I was a kid. Watching him with Della never ceased to amaze me. He hadn't been the settling-down type. But Della was his world.

"Coming right up," Della replied.

I didn't scan the inside of the jet, but I felt his eyes as soon as they found me. Tripp was here. The pressure of his gaze made things difficult. Uncomfortable. I didn't want to feel anything where he was concerned.

"Bethy," Harlow's voice called out in a pleasant greeting, and I turned to see her sitting on one of the leather sofas that lined the inside of the plane. She wasn't holding Lila Kate. I hadn't expected her to leave her baby behind, too. Especially since she was still so tiny. She was four months old now but she had been a preemie. She was a little thing, but she was so perfect. Just like her mother.

I walked over to sit down beside Harlow. "Where's Lila Kate?" I asked. I hadn't been by to visit her lately, either. Harlow nodded her head to the left of the plane, and I glanced over to see Grant standing by the bar with his little girl in his arms as he rocked her gently and talked softly to her.

"He's getting her to sleep. I had to beg him to bring her on the plane. He was completely freaked out by the idea of her flying. But then it took him a month to get over putting her in a car. I doubt anyone else will get to hold her while we're in the sky. Not even me," she said with an amused laugh.

Watching Grant hold his little girl so carefully and protectively, I remembered the man standing in the hospital, staring at the door that Harlow had been rushed through when she went into labor. He had stood there lost and unmoving for hours. It had been hard for everyone—I'd felt like I was losing Jace all over again—but Grant was a mess. I didn't pray often, but that week, I had prayed hard. "That's adorable," I said.

"God, isn't it, though? I swear, when he does that kind of stuff, I want to attack him. Complete turn-on."

I laughed, and it was a real laugh. It felt good. I missed laughing. I didn't do it often. Nate gave me my weekly laugh. He always made me forget with his little-boy charm.

"What's so funny over here?" Blaire asked, taking the seat on the other side of me.

"Daddy Grant is a turn-on for Harlow," I said with a chuckle, glancing over at her.

Blaire smiled as she looked over at Grant, who now had his head tucked close to Lila Kate as he continued to rock back and forth with her. "He's so stinking cute. I swear. I can't imagine Rush with a baby girl. But seeing Grant with Lila Kate makes me want one."

"Another baby so soon?" Harlow asked Blaire.

Blaire smiled and shrugged. "Maybe not yet. Nate still needs to be the baby a while longer. Besides, he's a handful. The walking thing was hard, but the running thing is even more difficult. I can't catch him when he gets loose."

I needed this. I sat as my friends discussed their children and told stories about their daily lives as moms, making me laugh. I loved them and their families. For almost two years, I had missed so much, closing myself off from emotion. I was tired of that. Maybe the protective numbness leaving was a good thing.

Tripp

Bethy had become an addiction. Although I knew I couldn't have her, I couldn't stay away from her. Seeing her face light up when she saw me was also pretty damn amazing. After she rode on the back of my bike that weekend all the way to New Orleans and back, I came up with reasons to see her every day. Jace kept asking me to hang out with him and the guys, but I couldn't bring myself not to see Bethy. The idea that she'd end up at another party and I wouldn't be there to protect her was also keeping me from giving her much space.

She didn't seem to mind. Hell, she looked at me like I was the only person she wanted to see. That felt pretty damn good. I was aware that she had a crush on me. It was too obvious to miss. It was becoming increasingly hard not to touch her. I really wanted to touch her. But right now, I'd settle for a kiss.

I sat outside her trailer on my bike, waiting for her. She didn't want me coming to the door, and although I didn't like it, I honored her wishes and waited on my bike. We were going

55

to Destin tonight for a summer jam concert I'd gotten tickets to. Several bands would be there that she and I both liked.

The door to her beat-to-hell trailer opened up, and she came running out wearing a short little sundress that show-cased her hot body. I was a goner. I swear, I was ready to break. Keeping my hands off her in that outfit was going to be impos-sible. Guys were gonna stare at her tonight, and I'd be damned if I let them think she was available.

She stopped and looked up at me as she got to the bike. "I was going to wear shorts because of the bike, but I have my bikini on under here, and I figured it would be OK to wear this." She seemed nervous. We'd spent so much time together over the past two weeks I wasn't sure how she could still be so uncertain around me.

"I like the dress," I assured her, holding out my hand to help her climb on back. Then I handed her the helmet I kept just for her.

"You have to be home at a certain time?" I asked, already knowing the answer was probably a no. Her father wasn't home much. Only when she was at her aunt Darla's did she have a curfew.

"Nope. Dad won't be home tonight," she replied, slipping her arms around my waist and pressing her chest against my back. That never got old. Feeling her tits up against me was part of the addiction I'd developed.

"Good. You're mine for the night," I replied before starting the bike and pulling out onto the road. I glanced down to see her naked legs locked around mine, and I had to take a deep breath. That was nice. Too damn nice.

I would speed up at times just to hear her squeal and

squeeze me tighter. Thinking about giving her up at the end of the summer was bothering me. Who would be here to take care of her? She was so sweet and innocent. I couldn't stand the idea of someone hurting her or taking advantage of her. And if I was honest with myself, I hated the idea of anyone else touching her. I had no claim on her, but it felt like she was mine.

When she looked up at me with those adoring eyes, all was right with the world. She belonged to me then. I knew it by the way the stars in her eyes only appeared for me. I had watched her with other guys while she worked, and no one got the same adoring gaze I got. That was just for me.

⌘

Once we got to the beach where the concert was being held, I found us a spot and laid out the blanket I had brought. I figured we would be standing most of the night to see over the heads of everyone when the bands started playing, but right now, we had more than an hour before the show got started. People were sprawled all over the place on their own blankets and chairs, drinking and partying.

Bethy sank down beside me but left some space between us. I didn't like it, but she always gave me space. As if she were afraid I'd push her away if she got any closer. She was being smart. I just couldn't be smart any longer.

I reached over and hooked my hand around her waist and pulled her up against me until her leg was touching mine and her side was pressed up against me. She made a surprised sound but didn't try to move away. But then I knew she wouldn't.

"You look beautiful tonight," I told her.

Just like always, she blushed at my compliment. "Thank you," she replied softly.

I kept my hand on her waist and began tracing little circles with my finger against her side. She stiffened at first, but then she shivered. That was my breaking point. "Come here," I said, then moved her to straddle me. Her eyes went wide as she sat on my lap facing me. I cupped her face before I could change my mind and covered her mouth with mine.

She inhaled sharply, and for a moment, she didn't react. Then her hands were in my hair as I slipped my tongue along her bottom lip. She opened for me slowly, and I dove in, ready to taste her. The feel of her honey-sweet warmth made *me* shiver this time. It was better than I'd expected. I slid my hands under her dress to feel her bare skin as she made a soft moaning noise and leaned closer into me.

Fuck, this was good. No, this was perfect. This was one of those kisses that changed everything. I wanted to feel more of her, but we were on a public beach, and I didn't like the idea of other guys watching what was mine.

When she arched her back, pressing her breasts against my chest for friction, I broke the kiss before I lost control and put my hands on her tits, which I'd been using as inspiration daily.

Bethy's face was flushed, and she was breathing hard as I pulled away from her. She looked dazed, and I wanted to roar with pleasure that I'd put that look there. I held her close to me as I caught my own breath. Her eyes flickered from mine to my lips and back.

She let out a long breath and sank down onto my lap. My erection greeted her, and she stilled. The fact that she was straddling my dick was not helping me calm down. "Don't move, baby," I told her through gritted teeth. I reminded myself that other guys could see this. I didn't like them seeing her like this. It was the only reason I managed to pick her up and move her off of me. The urge to press against her center was intense. But not here. I couldn't do that here.

"I'm sorry," she whispered. I glanced down at her face. She looked worried and embarrassed. Shit.

I kept her close to my side. Bending my head so that my mouth was at her ear, I pressed a kiss to the side of her neck. "Don't ever say you're sorry for that."

She studied me a moment before replying. "OK."

Bethy

Something changed that night. After that kiss, Tripp's hands were all over me, and he wouldn't let me move away from him. It was the most wonderful feeling in the world. I wanted him to kiss me again. I had been kissed before but not like that. Never like that.

The sun had set, and in the darkness, Tripp pulled me closer. His hands were under my dress now and resting on my stomach. His touch on my bare skin felt like an electric current coursing through me. I had no idea who was singing or what they were saying. My eyes were closed as I leaned against Tripp, and I felt his hardness against my back. When I had sunk down on it, I'd had to bite back a cry of pleasure. The sensation between my legs was new, but he'd moved me fast.

His hands slowly moved up until they rested just under my breasts. I breathed hard. I couldn't help it. With each breath, his thumb brushed the underside of my bikini top. Unable even to pretend I was listening to the band, I laid my head back against his chest and inhaled shakily.

"What's wrong?" he asked close to my ear. "Is this OK?"

I wanted to scream *God, yes!* But I didn't. I simply nodded. Tonight things had taken a drastic turn. I had been convincing myself that Tripp saw me as a friend and nothing more. Then he'd kissed me. Telling myself that he just wanted to be my friend was impossible now. My infatuation was full-blown. I couldn't hide it anymore.

"Can we go now?" he asked, moving his hands from their resting spot. I wanted to groan in protest. He was so close. The tingling in my body had been doing things between my legs again. It was driving me slightly crazy.

I managed another nod. Tripp picked up the blanket and threw it over his arm, then grabbed my hand and pulled me through the crowd. His height made it easy for him to navigate through the bodies, since he was taller than most of them. I wasn't ready to go home, but the idea of getting to press my very needy body against his for the next hour sounded wonderful. Maybe I could find some relief then.

It wasn't until we were out of the crowd that I realized we weren't going to the parking lot where we had left his bike. We were going farther away from the beach to the stretch ahead where there were no condos or houses.

It was dark, and I watched for crabs as we walked farther away from the noise. My heartbeat picked up and the butterflies in my stomach started fluttering again as we headed into the darkness of the deserted beach. We walked under a bridge, and Tripp stopped and threw the blanket down before looking at me.

"Come here, Bethy," he said. His eyes were hard to see in the darkness, but I didn't question him. I was pretty sure that if he asked me to jump off that bridge into the dark water, I would.

He reached for the hem of my dress and pulled it off, then

dropped it onto the blanket. "I can't promise you anything, Bethy. And I shouldn't touch you. But I want to so damn bad. Tell me to stop, and I will, sweetheart."

Tell him to stop? Not in this lifetime. I didn't say anything.

"Do you want me to touch you?" he asked in a whisper as he reached out and pulled me closer to him.

I managed a nod this time.

He dropped his head, buried his face in the curve of my neck, and muttered a curse. The warmth of his breath caused me to shiver, and I stepped closer to him. "You're so beautiful. It hurts to look at you and not touch you," he said against my neck, then placed a kiss there. "I've tried to fight this. I just want to keep you safe. Even from me," he said again as his mouth moved to kiss my jawline.

I didn't want to be protected from him. Ever. "I don't want to be safe from you," I said. Before I could lose the nerve, I reached up and untied my bikini top and took a breath as we both froze. It would fall down and expose me the moment one of us moved. I wanted his hands on me. I wasn't scared of Tripp. I was in love with him.

Tripp moved first, and I closed my eyes as the top of my swimsuit fell down, leaving the breeze to dance across my bare breasts.

"Holy fuck," Tripp whispered with awe in his voice, which made my nipples tighten up and the tingle between my legs ignite again.

It felt like forever before his large, warm hands covered me. The feel of his palm against me made me cry out his name as I reached to grab hold of his arms. I wasn't sure I could remain standing if he did much more.

He ran his thumbs over my tender area. My legs wobbled, and I held on tighter, gripping his hands. "Look at me, Bethy," he said in a hoarse whisper. I forced my eyes open, knowing he was going to see everything I was feeling reflected in them. I wasn't able to hide my feelings for him anymore. Not like this.

His hands moved from my breasts. I started to protest before I could stop myself, but he pulled me against him as he reached around and undid the back of my suit so that my top no longer hung there but fell to the sand below. Then his hands were back on me, holding the weight of my breasts as he looked at them with reverence. I trembled, and his eyes looked back up at me.

"Do you trust me?" he asked.

"Yes," I breathed out. The desperate sound in my voice should have been embarrassing, but it wasn't. Not when he was looking at me like that.

He lowered his head and covered my mouth with his again. The minty taste of him made my knees weak. I grabbed his arms again, and a growl came from his chest before he pulled back and then took me down to the blanket with him. "Straddle me again," he said, moving me over his lap. I was careful not to sink down onto him again. I didn't want to end this. But he grabbed my hips and pushed me down until my center was tightly pressed against his hardness. "Fuck," he groaned, and I realized it felt good to him, too. I'd thought he had stopped earlier because he didn't like it.

I was relieved, because this friction felt better than anything we'd done so far. I relaxed into his lap. Tripp kissed my mouth again, but then his mouth was moving down my neck, his lips brushing across my collarbone. My breasts were aching so badly. Seeing his mouth so close was too much.

Before I could break down and whimper, his mouth moved lower, and he pressed a kiss to one of my puckered nipples before pulling it into his hot mouth. The sensation that followed sent a string of fireworks off in my body. I grabbed his head and held him there. This was heaven, and I didn't want him to stop. Ever.

His teeth teased me, and then he sucked harder. I chanted his name, holding his head against me. When he moved to the other breast, I whimpered in relief. This was amazing. His hips moved under me, and the other part of my body woke up again. The tingling in my breasts was joined with the one between my legs. I rocked against him, and he groaned as he continued to lavish my breasts with attention.

I took that as a good thing and began rocking on him again. With each rub of his hardness against me, I became more crazed. There was something there that I needed. "Tripp," I panted, not sure what it was I was trying to achieve, though I knew I wanted it.

He lifted his head from my chest and claimed my mouth again. I threw all my hunger into the kiss, wanting him as close to me as possible. He pulled back for a second and jerked his shirt over his head before returning to our kiss. My wet, sensitive nipples were pressed up against his chest, and I wanted to weep with joy.

I needed him closer. I rubbed against him harder, and my breathing became erratic. I had to get there. I couldn't control myself. There was a need inside me taking over everything else.

Then Tripp's hand slipped inside my bikini bottoms, and I stopped moving and sucked in a breath. He was going to touch me. There. Oh, God.

"Trust me," he said again, as if reminding me.

I nodded, but I didn't breathe. When his finger slid along my folds, my entire body jerked in response. "Oh, God!" I cried out, unable to contain myself.

"Shhh. Easy, baby. I got you," he said in my ear as he held me against him. His breathing was heavy and as fast as mine. "You're soaking wet," he said as his finger slid easily along me, because he was right: I was wet.

I ducked my head, suddenly embarrassed. Was I supposed to be wet? Was he grossed out?

"Bethy, sweetheart, look at me," he said, using his free hand to tilt my chin up. I forced myself to do as he asked, and the heat in his eyes made my breath catch.

"The fact that you're wet for me is so sexy. It means you want me as much as I want you, and nothing could ever be sweeter than that. Ever," he said, then slipped a finger inside me.

At that moment, I would believe anything he said. "I want to taste you, here," he said, sliding his finger back out of me. I had heard about that. I knew people did it, but I wasn't sure why. "Can I taste you? Will you let me?" he asked, his voice strained. I wanted him to enjoy this as much as I was. If he wanted to taste me, then I'd let him.

I nodded, and he moved me fast. I was on my back as he pulled my bottoms down my legs. I was completely naked. No guy had ever seen me naked. I was suddenly very nervous.

Tripp didn't notice, though. His focus was completely on

my most private area. He pushed my thighs open, and the light in his eyes got brighter. That could not be attractive down there. Why did he seem to like it so much?

He lowered himself until his head was between my legs. His finger was on me again, but this was different. I was completely open to him. Not hidden under my bottoms. "You're even beautiful here," he said in a soft whisper as he ran a finger slowly down until it met with the opening it had entered earlier.

"Ahhh, Tripp," I said as my hips bucked involuntarily from the touch of his finger.

"Mmm-hmm," he replied before the heat of his tongue touched me.

"Aaahhhhh!" I screamed at the contact. It was so much better than feeling his finger, which I thought would be impossible.

"Tastes better than I imagined," he said against my heated flesh, then licked me again. I couldn't breathe. I was lost. This was too much and not enough.

Tripp's mouth began to taste me with wild abandon as he slipped his tongue inside me, then back up, circling the most sensitive area there. Each time he touched that one spot, I cried out his name. I couldn't stop myself.

The growing feeling inside me escalated, and I knew I wanted whatever it was. If I died from this, I'd be OK with that. It was worth it. I just wanted more. I felt as if I was about to fall, and I wasn't sure where.

"Tripp," I said, grabbing at his shoulders.

"Come for me, sweetheart. I want to taste it," he said as his hand moved up my body to cup my breast.

I exploded, or at least the world around me did.

Tripp

Present day

She hadn't looked over at me once. It was deliberate, too. Smiling to myself, I stopped watching her so closely and turned my attention to Woods as he took a seat beside me. "You good?" he asked me. This was a regular question from Woods. Especially since I'd told him about my past with Bethy.

"Yeah," I replied, not wanting to put a damper on his weekend. "You ready to get hitched?"

Woods grinned and turned his gaze to Della, who was standing at the bar fixing herself a glass of water. "More than anything in my life. I'd have married her sooner had she let me. But Della deserves a fairy-tale wedding. I wanted to give her that."

Della turned to look at Woods as if she knew we were talking about her and smiled at him sweetly.

He slapped my knee and stood up. "Good chatting with you, but I've got to talk to my beautiful fiancée in the back room about something."

Woods was gone before I could reply. He wasn't taking her

into the back room to talk. Chuckling, I turned my attention back to Bethy, who was sitting between Harlow and Blaire. Smiling. Really smiling. She was happy. Whatever they were talking about made her smile. I had missed that smile so damn much. She never smiled for me now.

Grant moved over to sit down beside Harlow, with his baby girl tucked close to his chest. Harlow said something to him, and he grinned and leaned over to press a kiss to her lips. I watched Bethy as she took in their happiness. There wasn't resentment in her face. But there was longing. It made me ache. I hated knowing Bethy was alone. I hated that she wouldn't let me near her.

The pilot came over the speaker and told everyone to prepare for takeoff. Rush walked over and took Blaire's hand, pulling her with him to sit in a more private area. Bethy looked lost in that moment. Like she wasn't sure where she fit in now.

Thad took the now-vacated seat beside her and said something to make her smile. I wanted to knock his pretty-boy teeth down his throat and thank him at the same time. He'd seen what I had seen, and he'd gone in to fix it. She would let him. *He* hadn't broken her heart.

I leaned back in my seat and buckled my seat belt like everyone else. I rested my head against the back of the seat and closed my eyes. I couldn't sit here and watch Thad entertain Bethy for the next two hours. I was glad he was there for her, but watching it was too hard.

封

When Della and Woods had told everyone we would all be put up in our own private huts, I had expected something less luxurious. This was far from a hut. I stood inside a small house that sat directly on the clear blue water. There was a walkway to the main part of the island and to the other "huts." Stone walls and a fireplace were only part of the surprising accommodations. The entire house was open on all four sides, giving me a water view wherever I looked. At night, the walls came down at the touch of a button.

The king-size bed that sat in the center of the room was surrounded by white gauzy shit that hung from the ceiling. I set my duffel bag on the bed and walked out to the water to get a good look at my surroundings. This was definitely a fairy tale. Woods hadn't been kidding. He'd gone all out.

Movement to my left caught my attention, and I turned to see Bethy walking out of the next hut over, wearing a bikini. She hadn't noticed me yet, so I stepped back inside, just out of sight. I watched as she coated herself with sunscreen before lying down on the double-teak lounger. There were only two huts on each of the twenty extensions from the island. My only neighbor was Bethy. She wasn't going to like this, but I wasn't going to let her know right away. I'd wait until it was too late for her to ask for another hut.

I sat down on the glorified beanbag chair inside so I could watch her without her seeing me. She glanced around once, and I grinned from my hidden spot. Then she turned over and untied her top. Fuck. I couldn't see her, but just knowing I'd get a view of her tits if she sat up was enough to keep me on edge. I silently prayed she would have to reach for something. Soon.

She had undone her bikini straps for me once. But I'd lost that girl, along with her adoring gazes. Pain sliced through my chest whenever I thought of never having that again. I wasn't going to lie, I had looked for it elsewhere. When I knew I would never have Bethy again, I had tried to recapture that feeling I'd had with her. I had tried with so many women. But even the ones with stars in their eyes never measured up. They weren't Bethy.

It had taken me six long years to face the fact that I would only ever want her. Coming back to Rosemary Beach and seeing her with Jace, I had told myself her happiness would be enough for me. But it hadn't been. I had wanted more. So I'd left Rosemary Beach again, not wanting to ruin what she had with Jace.

But my leaving hadn't helped anything. It had only made things worse.

I never should have returned. But I had, and I couldn't change that now.

I wasn't leaving Bethy again.

Bethy

This was easier than I'd expected. The peace and quiet were perfect. I felt the warmth from the day's sun on my arms and legs as I walked toward the luau on the main part of the island. This wasn't the rehearsal dinner—that would be tomorrow night. This was Della and Woods's version of a bachelor and bachelorette party. Woods had been adamant about not having one, and he didn't want Della to have one, either. He wanted to party with their friends as a couple, not celebrate apart. So we were doing it island-style at a luau. The coconut tops and authentic grass skirts that Della had delivered to our huts were a surprise. I had to admit they were more comfortable than I'd imagined. I was glad I'd gotten some sun on my arms before putting on the top.

Tiki torches lit the way as I walked toward the gathering crowd.

"Hello, Bethy." Tripp's voice startled me, and I turned to see him; he was wearing a pair of board shorts and nothing else. He had several tattoos now. I didn't want to study them or admire them, so I tore my gaze off his naked chest and turned back around.

"Hi," I replied coolly. Ignoring him on this island would

be uncomfortable for everyone. I didn't want that for Woods and Della. It was time I moved past this and ended all emotion where Tripp was concerned.

As if he had read my thoughts, he gave me space and didn't say another word. We walked in silence toward the group, and then Tripp walked off to the right to the bar without a backward glance my way.

Letting out the breath I'd been holding, I went in the opposite direction and found Blaire sipping a fruity drink and talking to Della.

"Rush is a very big fan of the outfit. He said he was eternally grateful to you," Blaire was saying, giggling, as I walked up. I could only imagine how excited Rush was about the coconut bra and the grass skirt Blaire was wearing.

"Hello, Bethy," Della said through her laughter. "It appears the men are very happy with the ladies' outfits tonight. Well, except for Grant. Harlow texted me that she was having a hard time getting out of the hut in it. Grant was being a caveman about her wearing it in public."

That sounded like Grant. He'd been all fun and games until Harlow walked into his life. Now he was a protective daddy and a possessive husband. It looked good on him.

"So how do you like your hut?" Della asked, watching me carefully. As if she were prepared for me not to love it.

"I think it's fabulous. So not a hut, more like a personal paradise on water."

Della glanced over my shoulder and then back at me and smiled. "Good. I'm glad you're happy. We've filled up every hut on the island. I want everyone to be happy with their accommodations."

"Seriously. This place is amazing," I assured her.

"Rush and I are staying on the main island," Blaire said, taking a sip of her drink. "Those huts look fabulous, but once Nate gets here, I wouldn't be able to sleep thinking about him running off into the water so easily. But the hut they gave us on the main island is beautiful. We love it, and it's far enough off the water that I won't be nervous about Nate taking a flying leap into it."

Blaire glanced over my shoulder, then looked back at me with a frown. "Bethy, what's going on with you and Tripp?" she asked. Leave it to Blaire to just ask me straight out. I had dodged this question with her so many times I couldn't count anymore.

"Nothing," I replied, feeling guilty for not telling her the truth.

"You're lying to me. I can see it all over your face. Plus, Tripp watches your every move."

Della had a nervous look on her face. She knew something. She and Tripp were friends. Good friends. He'd been the reason she came to Rosemary Beach in the first place. I had been so incredibly jealous of her. I had hated myself for it, too. Pretending it hadn't been killing me when she'd stayed at Tripp's condo had been hard. But then it hadn't been but a couple of weeks before it was obvious that Della wanted Woods.

"Bethy, look at me," Blaire said in a low voice.

I glanced up at her, and the concerned frown on her face only deepened. "Did something happen with you and Tripp?"

I was tired of pretending it hadn't happened. "A long time ago. Before he left Rosemary Beach the first time," I admitted in a whisper.

Della let out a sigh, and I looked over at her to see relief on her face. She had known. He'd told her. But she hadn't said anything. Not even to Blaire.

"Thought so. That's the only thing that made sense," Blaire said, studying someone across the fire. I didn't have to look to know she was watching Tripp. "Was it serious?"

"Yes," I replied. I couldn't tell her more. I couldn't tell either of them more. It was a secret that hurt too much to share. It was my biggest mistake. I would never forgive myself. Every time I held Nate and Lila Kate, I knew I would never be worthy of having kids. I couldn't forgive myself. How could I expect anyone else to?

"But it was a long time ago. Why are you so mad at him?" Blaire asked.

Because he made me question my love for Jace. Because he reminded me that I had something big once. Something huge. He reminded me that what I felt for Jace wasn't as big. And I hated myself for that. I hated him for it. "I can't talk about it. Please, just drop it," I said, unable to look at her.

I didn't wait for a response. I forced a smile at Della, then turned and headed away from the group. I wanted the darkness for a moment. To be alone. To pull myself together so I could go back and pretend I was OK.

I heard footsteps behind me and walked faster. Blaire wasn't one to back down. She'd be worried about me now. I just wished for once she'd back off. Let me deal with this alone.

"No, Blaire. I got this," Tripp's voice said, stopping me in place.

No one spoke. I wasn't sure if I should run and cause a

scene or deal with this. Facing Blaire was easier than facing Tripp.

"Don't push her," Tripp said in a stern tone.

Blaire let out a frustrated sigh. "She needs to talk to someone."

"And it doesn't have to be you. She will when she's ready. Leave her alone." Tripp's tone with Blaire surprised me. I turned around to look at Blaire, who was locked in a staring contest with Tripp.

"Fine. But I'm not sure she wants you, either," Blaire said.

"She doesn't. But I'm not pushing her to talk." Tripp took a step to place himself between Blaire and me. I didn't need protection from my best friend, but the wall I'd built suffered a small crack with that one move.

Blaire nodded and walked back to the party.

When she was out of sight, Tripp turned around, and our gazes locked. "You OK?" he asked.

I tried to nod, but I only managed a shrug.

"That's not convincing, Bethy."

I had been lying to everyone for so long I was out of lies. I was tired of it. No, I wasn't OK. I was a horrible person. I had to live with that. I had to live with the pain and destruction I had caused. I would never be OK. "Thanks for . . ." I waved my hand toward where Blaire stood. "That," I finished.

He nodded. Then he turned and walked away. He wasn't going to stay and make me talk. Another small crack in my wall. This wasn't good. I needed my wall now more than ever.

Tripp

Bethy came back to the luau fifteen minutes later with a smile that didn't match her eyes, but no one seemed to notice but me. She danced with Thad and then a bit with Blaire. She held Lila Kate for a while. Seeing her talk to the baby and cuddle her in her arms hurt. I couldn't look away, even though the pain of what we had lost was breathtaking. I didn't blame Bethy. She'd been young and scared. Her father was never happy with her and was rarely around. She hadn't been ready to be a mother then. And I hadn't been there to stand beside her.

But I did blame me. Forgiving others was easy—it was forgiving myself that was proving impossible.

One of the servers who kept coming back to flirt with me appeared at my arm again. "I get off in five minutes," she said close to my ear. The girl was younger than me by a couple of years. Her long blond hair stood out against her island tan. There was no question that she was attractive. Thad had been watching her all night. But she'd kept coming over to me.

"I'm sure you're tired," I replied evenly, not taking my eyes off Bethy. She was handing Lila Kate back to her daddy. Grant didn't let that kid out of his arms often.

"I'm actually ready for some fun. A late-night swim, maybe,

if I had some company," she said as she ran her hand up my arm. She was tracing one of my tattoos. It was the first ink I got, and women seemed to love it best. What they didn't realize was that inside the tribal print that covered most of my left arm were roman numerals marking the date most important to me.

"Do you see the date hidden in the print?" I asked the girl, not looking at her. I wanted to see if Bethy was leaving.

"Hmmm . . . here?" she asked, tracing the numerals.

"Yeah," I said as Bethy laughed at something Thad was saying to her. It was forced. She didn't feel it. I knew the sound of her real laugh.

"Six, twenty-eight, two thousand and eight," she said as her finger traced the last number. "What does it represent? Can't be your birthday," she said teasingly.

"It was the night I gave my heart to that woman over there," I said simply.

The night Bethy had become mine.

The girl's finger stopped tracing the ink and fell away. She didn't speak at first. I thought she'd walk away now. I expected her to.

"She hasn't spoken to you all night. I thought you were single," the server finally said.

"She has hated me for eight years. Doesn't change anything," I replied.

As if she could hear me from across the fire, Bethy's gaze lifted and met mine. I watched as her chest rose and fell quickly. She shifted her eyes to the girl beside me before turning away. Her suddenly stiff posture didn't worry me. In fact, I wanted to shout and pound my chest. Bethy was jealous. Or at least, she was affected by seeing me with someone else.

It was a start.

"She doesn't look interested," the girl said.

"Doesn't change anything," I repeated. Because it didn't. I was done with shallow and meaningless.

The girl sighed and finally stepped away from me. "That's a shame. We could have had fun."

No. We could have had empty.

I let her walk away without acknowledging her last attempt to get my attention. Bethy didn't look back at me. When she started to move, I took a step in that direction, too.

Before I could take another one, though, a hand landed on my shoulder. Turning back, I saw Rush standing there, and I wondered if he was here to try to kick my ass for talking to his wife the way I had earlier.

"Bethy," he said, and I didn't reply, because I wasn't sure what he meant. "I heard what you told the server. The date on your arm. That was the summer before you left. You were talking about Bethy."

"Yeah," I mumbled, but I didn't stick around to answer any more questions. Bethy was headed for her hut out on the water.

"Well, now it all makes fucking sense," Rush muttered as I walked away.

Bethy didn't seem to notice she was being followed. She kept her head down as she walked out over the water and passed my hut. I watched her glance at it, and I wondered if it had even occurred to her to see who was staying next door.

I walked up to my hut and stopped as she stood outside hers. She crossed her arms over her stomach as she looked out over the water. I moved behind the shade of the palm tree outside my door and watched as she let her head fall back and closed her eyes. I wished I could get her to talk to me. I wanted to tell her so much. I wanted to hold her and mourn what we had lost together. But more than anything, I wanted her in my life. Any way she'd allow.

"I know you're there. You're always there. I don't know what to do with that, Tripp. I don't know what to do about anything anymore." Bethy's words snapped me out of my inner thoughts, and I stepped out of what I thought was my hiding place.

She turned to look at me with so much pain in her eyes. I wanted to heal that. Take it away. "Talk to me," I said.

Bethy shook her head and looked away. "Anything we'd say would hold so much hurt. Why do you want to bring it all up again?"

"It's the first step to healing. And not everything is painful," I reminded her. Because it wasn't. We had memories that got me through some of the hardest times.

"You want that girl you left behind. I'm not her! Don't you get it? She's gone. I've lost her. I made choices that made me an awful person. I'm not worth all this time and energy you're wasting."

Fuck. I took a step toward her, and she took a step back. "You're wrong there. I don't want the sixteen-year-old girl I left behind. I want the woman she's become. The kind, compassionate, faithful, strong woman I watch from afar every day of my life. I want her. Nothing ever changed for me. Not with you."

Bethy let out a hard laugh that made me wince. It was laced with pain and anger. "I aborted my baby, Tripp. Our baby. Then I slept with guys who didn't give a shit about me. Until Jace saw something worthwhile in me. He loved me. Then you walked back into Rosemary Beach, and my stupid heart picked up and came back to life. Jace loved me and wanted a life with me, but *you* were invading my dreams and thoughts.

I can't take that back. He's gone, and I can't make it right—"

"Stop. You were a kid, Bethy. A scared kid. And you did the only thing you knew to do. What your aunt wanted you to do. That decision was all my fault. All me, sweetheart. It was all me. That's my cross to bear. Not yours. You slept with guys because you were trying to cover the pain. And Jace was smart enough to see the beauty inside you and want that in his life. You're easy to love, Bethy. So damn easy to love. Jace got that. He loved you, and you loved him. Me coming back to town brought up old memories and things you wanted to forget. You didn't betray Jace. You loved him. I was just a part of your past that you didn't have closure on. So don't blame yourself. Don't think you did something wrong."

Bethy's tear-streaked face turned toward me. Her look told me that I was right, that I hadn't been her only love. It was something I tried not to think about, because she was it for me. I'd never felt that way about anyone else. But she had. Her heart had moved on.

"I did love him," she said with a sad smile. "I loved him so much. But when I saw you again, there was something in me that woke up. That's something I have to live with. He deserved all of me, and he never had that."

I didn't have a response for that. Bethy turned and walked into her hut. I didn't move. I stood there for what seemed like forever, staring at the spot she'd been standing in.

She had loved Jace. I'd seen it in her eyes when she looked at him. He had made her happy. Every time he told her he loved her and she melted into his arms, my soul had shattered a little more.

But was she telling me that I still had a piece of her heart?

Bethy

When I left for the bridesmaids' breakfast and spa treatments on the main island the next morning, Tripp's walls were still down on his hut. I figured he was still sleeping. I had expected him to show up at my door last night after what I'd said. But he hadn't. He wasn't going to push me. He had always wanted to protect me. Even from himself. That was one of the things I'd loved about him when I was a young girl.

No one had really ever wanted to protect me besides Aunt Darla, and sometimes she didn't do a very good job. But Tripp had been my hero back then. He had cared about me, and he'd made sure I knew it. His actions were all I needed. He was doing that still.

I felt another crack in my wall. Damn, my wall was weakening fast. What would I do when it finally crumbled? How would I deal? Maybe we needed closure. Then we could move on. Find a life where we could start over fresh. Where old memories didn't haunt us.

"Bethy!" Blaire called out my name, and I turned to see her hurrying toward me. She was wearing a designer sundress and a pair of heels. Both of which cost more than my entire wardrobe. Seeing her all dolled up made me smile. I remembered the girl in jeans and tank tops.

"Good morning," I said as she caught up with me. "You look like you're ready to walk down a runway. Per usual."

Blaire grimaced. "I know. Rush makes me spend money on clothes. It's part of his taking-care-of-me thing. I do it for him."

"Don't make excuses. Own your sexy self," I teased.

Blaire frowned and took my hand in hers, getting serious on me fast. I didn't want to hash this out with her, but knowing Blaire, it had bothered her all night. I needed to let her talk so she could feel better. "I'm sorry about last night."

I nodded. "Me, too. I was having a bad moment."

Blaire took a deep breath. "I don't want to make you tell me something you don't want to. But I'm here when you're ready to talk about . . . things. Tripp."

Last night, we'd been too obvious. At least to Blaire. Slowly, our friends were starting to question our past. But talking about it would mean we'd have to tell them everything.

I wasn't ready.

"Thank you. And when I can deal with it, I will come to you first. But before that, Tripp and I have to deal with things. Things from the past. We haven't done that. I just haven't been ready. Part of me expected him to leave and give up. But deep down, the part of me who knows him knew he wouldn't leave."

Blaire pressed her lips together tightly, as if trying to hold back a million questions. She finally nodded and pulled me into a hug. "I love you. I'm here. OK?"

Tears pricked my eyes. "Love you, too," I croaked out.

When she pulled back, she sniffed and blinked away her own tears, then smiled. "Let's go celebrate with Della."

"Yeah. I'm starving. I hope this island breakfast is damn good."

Blaire laughed as she hooked her arm through mine. "Nate will be here tonight. He'll be thrilled to see his 'An Betty,'" she said as she patted my arm.

His Aunt Bethy was ready to see him, too.

Tripp

Eight years ago

Bethy hadn't been to my condo yet. We had spent most of our time together an hour out of town so no one could spot us. But tonight Bethy's dad was out of town, and I wasn't letting her stay alone. I had to hope like hell Woods and his friends didn't show up.

The idea of having Bethy in my bed, sleeping beside me, made any risk I took worth it. I had her overnight bag on my arm as I opened my condo and motioned her inside. She walked in slowly and looked around. It wasn't that big, but it was nicer than where she lived. I knew that.

"You hungry?" I asked, slipping my hand to her lower back just because I needed to touch her.

She shook her head. "Not really. Can you see the Gulf from there?" she asked, pointing to the French doors leading outside to the balcony.

"Yep," I replied, setting her bag down on a bar stool and leading her to the doors so she could see for herself.

"This is really nice, Tripp," she said, glancing back at me in awe.

"Yeah, my grandfather is generous," I agreed. "My parents hate him for this, though," I added with a smile.

She stepped outside. "This is a fantastic view."

Her long dark hair was caught up in the breeze, and the moonlight illuminated her features. She was right. The view was amazing. I walked over and stretched out on the lounger and held my hand up to her. "Come sit with me."

She came to me without pause. Since the night on the beach, she'd lost some of her nervous reserve with me. I hadn't done more than kiss and touch her the past week, but that was only because I wasn't sure I could stop things if I let them get that far again.

I wrapped my arms around her and settled her between my legs so she could lie back against me. Just having her in my arms was enough. Most of the time. Other times I needed to touch her and watch her face as I made her feel good. She was so expressive. I craved that. Although I left most nights in serious pain. I had to get my own release. I couldn't ask her to do that.

"You sure you're not thirsty or anything?" I asked her as I drew circles with my finger over her arms. I just liked touching her.

"I'm good," she replied, snuggling closer against me. "I could stay like this forever."

Me, too. Having her with me, not having to share her with the world, was perfect. I didn't want morning to come.

"It will be July in a week," she said softly. The sadness in her voice didn't go unnoticed.

"Yeah, it will. Summer is going by too fast," I replied. I didn't want to talk about my leaving. I wasn't ready for that. I didn't want to leave her.

She didn't say anything right away, but I knew she was thinking about the fall. When I had to go. Finally, she sighed and laid her head back on my shoulder. "I'm afraid I won't be able to get over you."

Her words snapped me out of my own sad thoughts. Why would she want to get over me? That wasn't in my plan. If she got over me, would she move on to another guy? Someone else who would touch her and bring her to orgasm? Fuck no. I tightened my hold on her. "Why do you have to get over me?" I asked, trying not to let the panic I was feeling come through in my words.

She turned her head and looked up at me. "You'll move on, too. I'll just be a summer memory."

Bethy would never be just a summer memory. I wasn't willing to label this thing we had, but I knew I wasn't sharing. And if someone else touched her, I'd break his hands. The need to make sure she understood she was mine and always would be was irrational. Because I would leave in the fall. I had to. My future wasn't in Rosemary Beach, and she was too young to go with me.

"I don't want you to move on," I told her truthfully as I slipped my hand under her shirt. Bethy's breathing hitched as I covered one of her breasts with my hand. "I don't like the idea of someone else touching you."

She let out a ragged sigh, and I tugged down her bra so that her heaviness fell into my hands. She was motherfucking perfect. "Mmmm," she moaned, and arched into me.

"I just want to make you feel like this," I said, rolling a nipple between my finger and thumb. I slipped my other hand down the front of her shorts, and her legs fell open without hesitation. Smiling, I kissed the side of her head as I watched her eyelashes flutter closed.

Like always, Bethy was already so wet her panties were damp. She stayed like this with me. I'd touched other girls before like this. Girls before Bethy. They'd always been dry and tense. The idea of a wet pussy was incredibly hot. Until Bethy, I hadn't known what an already-wet one actually felt like. Then there was her smell. Just thinking about how she smelled made me hard.

She lifted her hips and whimpered as I slid a finger down to circle her clit. That was her favorite spot. I'd read enough magazines to learn how to do it just right.

"Take off your shorts and panties," I said. I wanted to watch my hand as I played with her. She lifted her bottom so I could help her tug them down. When they were gone, she lay back against me again with her legs open. I lifted my hand to smell her and licked the taste off my fingers. She watched me with wide eyes, and the pulse in her neck quickened and throbbed. "You taste really good," I told her.

She took a swift breath and squirmed.

"Lean up. I want you naked," I instructed her, knowing this was a bad idea. I hadn't had her naked since the night on the beach, and I'd wanted inside her so bad that night. I knew she'd let me if I asked. But I couldn't do that to her. I was leaving. I didn't deserve her virginity. But damn, I wanted it to be mine.

She lifted her shirt and tossed it, and I made quick work of her bra.

Then she leaned back again, completely naked in my arms. It was the most humbling and erotic sight I'd ever seen. I had only slept with four girls and seen about seven naked, so my experience wasn't that great, especially compared with Rush, Grant, and Woods. But I knew that this time with Bethy would mark me. For life.

Bethy

"Do you trust me?" Tripp asked.

I knew by now that when he asked me that, he was about to do something new. I also knew that it was going to feel amazing. But it still made me nervous. I nodded and braced myself for what came next.

"Lean up one more time," he said. I did as I was told.

He pulled his shirt off, and I was relieved. I didn't like being the only one naked. But then, I'd never seen him naked. He always just took off his shirt. His hands went to his shorts, and I stopped breathing.

"I'm just undoing them. When we're doing things . . . it gets tight and uncomfortable down there. I need to give it some space," he said, watching me closely.

I nodded, but I still couldn't breathe. Not because I was scared of what he was going to do but because I wanted to see him so badly. I'd felt him through his jeans and shorts, but I'd never seen anything.

He unzipped his shorts and tugged them down. As I lifted my bare bottom, he kicked his shorts off, then reached for me to settle back between his legs. The only thing between my bottom and his erection was the thin cotton of his navy boxer briefs.

Oh, boy.

The hardness felt different without the buffer of his shorts. It was bigger than I thought. Which scared and excited me all at once.

"Bethy, sweetheart, relax. I just needed some space. My boxers are staying on. I swear." He thought I was worried that he was going to push me for sex. He wouldn't have to push very hard. I was at his mercy. If Tripp asked me to do something, I would do it. That was the simple, pathetic truth.

"I know," I assured him.

"Good, now lie back and let me touch you," he said in my ear as I eased back against him.

Watching him undress had excited me, and with my excitement came the dampness. It had spread to my inner thighs, and opening back up so he could see that was humiliating. Maybe I could say I needed to use the restroom. But then I'd have to run into his apartment naked. Not a good idea, either.

Tripp's hand was on my knee, and he started pushing my legs open again. I squeezed my eyes closed as I slowly gave in. When his hand moved back down there, he paused as he felt me. I wanted to crawl into a hole somewhere. "Oh, fuuuuck," he groaned, and his fingers started moving again. He slipped two inside me this time as his breathing picked up. "God, baby, just when I think it's not possible for me to get more turned on, you open up to me again, dripping like this. Jesus, Bethy. You're going to kill me."

I liked it when he said things like that. It sounded dirty, but I liked it. Tripp saying things like that, with his voice all husky, made my whole body hum. His other hand slipped down and touched my damp inner thigh, and he muttered another curse. "Even your thighs. Were you dripping down them?"

I didn't know how to answer that. I wasn't sure how it had happened.

"Was it me taking off my shorts?" he asked against my ear.

I couldn't really form words with him touching me down there with both hands now.

He slipped his fingers back inside me, and I moved against his hands. "I would slip in so damn easy. Do you have any idea how bad I want to be inside you? To know I'm buried inside you. That you're mine, and no one else can have what I have. You're so tight and hot. It would be the closest to heaven I'm ever gonna get."

Oh, God. Those words. I panted as he breathed hard in my ear. He held me open with one hand and slid his finger gently, back and forth, through the moisture with the other.

I was fighting to breathe.

"Straddle me, Bethy. I want to feel you like this," he said.

I lifted a leg, and he slid me up until I was directly over the obvious erection jutting forward, tenting his boxers. Then he lowered me slowly over it. My weight pushed it back down against his stomach. He threw his head back and groaned as I sank down on him completely. Seeing him like this only made me tingle even harder down below, which I knew meant I was just getting wetter.

"Fuck, I want to feel this without the boxers. Do you trust me?" he asked as he opened his eyes and looked up at me.

I nodded, because the truth was, if he wanted to be inside me, I would let him. I loved Tripp. There was no doubt in my mind that I would always love him. Even when he left, I would love him. Giving him my virginity was something I wanted to do.

"OK. We have to be careful. You're slippery, and I don't want to mess up."

I stood up and turned around as he pulled down his boxers, and I watched in fascination as his cock sprang free. It was big and thick, and the end was red and swollen-looking. I wanted to touch it, but I wasn't sure that would be OK, so I didn't ask.

His eyes were focused on where we were about to touch for the first time, and the veins in his neck were standing out. "Sit back down on me," he said as he held his hardness down so that it wasn't sticking up.

When I felt the heat of his skin make contact, I gasped and pressed down hard. Tripp's hands grabbed my waist and squeezed as he growled, then cursed. Explosions lit my body from within, and I needed more. I knew the peak I was headed for, and the idea of reaching it with our bodies so intimately touching made me dizzy with want.

I slowly rocked my hips so that I was sliding up and down the length of him. I wasn't touching the tip, but I was sliding along most of it, and it was amazing.

"Holy fuck," Tripp ground out through his teeth.

I pressed my forehead to his and looked directly in his eyes as I picked up the pace. I'd had his hands and his mouth touch me, but it didn't compare with this: seeing him lose control and fall into the same bliss he always sent me spiraling toward.

"God, Bethy," he breathed, then pulled my bottom lip into his mouth and sucked on it.

I rocked harder. His loud groan when I ran over the tip, so red it had to be sensitive, made me want to do it more.

"Slow down, baby. Please," he panted.

I couldn't slow down. I was so close. But I didn't get to slide over his tip again, because he was picking me up and carrying me inside. I landed on my back on his sofa, but he was over me instantly, his mouth devouring mine as I clawed at him to get closer. The tip touched me, and I let my legs fall open and lifted my hips so I could feel it again.

Tripp tore his mouth from mine with a frustrated sound, then grabbed his hard length in his hand. I watched as he ran the tip back and forth over my opening, then touched my sensitive spot with it before doing it again.

"So wet. I'd slide inside so easily," he said, almost so low I couldn't hear him. He lifted his head to look at me. "See how good that looks. You're all wet and swollen."

I was about to explode. I grabbed his arms and began chanting his name as I watched him pick up speed. I stopped breathing at some point, and then my world shot off into a million brilliant colors. Warmth coated my stomach, and I shivered as he shouted my name.

Blinking, I came back to earth and stared up at Tripp, dazed, as he stared down at my stomach. I followed his gaze to see white stuff all over me. Then I noticed one small drop still on the tip of his cock. He'd come. On me.

Smiling, I looked up at him, and his eyes lifted to meet mine. In that moment, I felt it. He didn't have to tell me. I just knew. Tripp loved me, too.

Tripp

Present day

It had been a long day, with Bethy's words replaying over and over in my head. All of the guys had eaten lunch with Woods, and then we'd spent the rest of the afternoon playing golf. Woods—not Rush—tried to talk to me about Bethy, which was a relief, since I didn't feel like giving someone else the full backstory just yet.

I needed a plan. One that involved more than me following her every day. Bethy was talking to me now. I had to figure out what the next move should be. Because her words last night weren't forgotten, nor would they ever be. They were the small ray of hope I'd been looking for.

I waited outside my hut for Bethy to come out of hers. We were due at rehearsal in ten minutes. Luckily, we weren't being forced to dress in tuxes tonight—the dress code was dressy casual. Slacks and a button-up shirt would suffice.

Bethy stepped out, fidgeting with her purse. Her gaze swung up to meet mine, and she faltered a moment. She hadn't been expecting me to wait for her. I had been doing the at-a-distance thing for so long now.

The pale yellow skirt she wore hit her at mid-thigh and was made from the type of flowy material that caught the breeze and teased you. She wore it with a sleeveless white blouse that tied at her waist and a pair of backless heels.

When I'd finished taking in every gorgeous inch of her, I lifted my eyes back up to meet hers. "You look beautiful."

I could see the emotion flash in her eyes before she tucked her purse under her arm and stiffened. "Thank you," she replied tightly.

"Did you enjoy your day at the spa?" I asked as she took a tentative step in my direction. She had to pass me to get to the rehearsal. There was no way around it. Unless she wanted to swim there.

"It was nice," she said.

Neither of us moved. It was a standoff.

Finally, Bethy sighed. "What do you want?"

I grinned, amused by her exasperated tone. "To walk with you to the rehearsal."

She started to say something, then closed her mouth. I watched her internal struggle. Finally, she caved. "Sure. Fine. Whatever."

She walked toward the island, and I fell in step beside her. I didn't push further by forcing her to talk to me. I decided this was enough for now. She wasn't shoving me in the water and screaming at me. We had made progress.

Everyone was gathering on the stretch of beach where the wedding would be held. When we reached the group, Bethy finally stopped walking and looked at me. "I'm tired of this. We were friends once. We both loved Jace, and we both lost him. I'm done trying to blame someone other than myself. I don't want to be angry anymore. It's time I rebuilt my life and found myself again. So"—she held out her hand toward me—"friends?"

Friends. We'd never be just friends. But if that was what she wanted to do, then I could work with it. I slipped my hand into hers, and we shook.

Then she smiled. A real, unforced Bethy smile. "This is a good thing. Jace would want this. Right?"

I shook her hand and let go as she pulled it away. "Yeah. He'd want this. He'd want to see you happy."

Bethy nodded. Then she turned and headed toward the group. I didn't follow her, though. Not yet. I had to let the moment soak in. Bethy was ready to forgive me. We were going to be friends.

I looked over to see Woods watching me. I nodded my head and grinned at him before making my way over to receive my instructions, along with the rest of the guys.

"There's the last one," Thad said, pointing at me as I walked up. The lady with her hair up in a bun and an iPad Mini in her hands looked like she was the boss.

"Height problem," she announced. "Della has you with Braden, but Braden is too short for you. Even with heels. Most women are too short for you, but Braden will be barefoot on the sand. It'll look bad. Let's see," she said, scanning something on her iPad. "Where's Bethy?" the lady asked.

"Yo, Bethy!" Thad called out, and Bethy turned to look over at us. "Come here."

She walked toward us, her skirt dancing in the breeze. I hated knowing Thad was admiring the view, too. I was going to have to set him straight.

"Yes. Much better. She's at least three inches taller. Not such a massive gap," the lady said as she looked at Bethy. "Thad, you will be escorting Braden. And Tripp, you will be escorting Bethy. Now, for your positions," she said, walking off with her back straight, pointing and barking commands at everyone in her wake.

"Yeah, but Tripp's the best man, and Braden is the maid of honor. Aren't they supposed to walk out together?" Thad asked. I shot a warning glare at him. If he had any intentions where Bethy was concerned, I'd remedy that real fast.

"This is my job. I'll make it work. I don't need your help," the lady snapped at Thad, who shut the hell up.

I glanced back at Bethy. "You good with this?" I asked her. I was fucking thrilled about it, but I didn't want to make her do something she didn't want to do. I'd deal with the drill sergeant if I had to.

She shrugged. "Sure. Friends, remember?" she replied matter-of-factly.

I watched the breeze play with her skirt as she walked away.

"Friends, huh?" Rush said, coming to stand beside me.

"Yeah. She's decided we can be friends," I told him, not taking my eyes off her. She said something to Della, who glanced over at us and then back at Bethy. I saw Bethy nod, and Della looked relieved.

"I tried the friends thing with Blaire once. It lasted less than a week before I was stripping her naked in the back of my Range Rover. Good luck with that," Rush said in an amused tone before walking off.

He didn't have the history with Blaire that I had with Bethy. It would take a hell of a lot longer before I made that kind of headway with Bethy.

He had no idea what I had to overcome with her.

Bethy

"An Betty, see me!" Nate's little voice called out. I spun around to see Nate in Rush's arms as they walked into the rehearsal dinner. Rush bent down to set his son on the floor, and then his little legs were off and heading straight for me. Laughing, I opened my arms for him.

"My best fella is here," I said as his little arms wrapped around my neck. Nate had been only a few months old when Jace drowned, and I'd spent a lot of time with Blaire during the months afterward. I couldn't be alone. Watching Nate when they'd needed a sitter had been good for me, and we'd bonded.

"I flew in da pwayne," he announced as I picked him up in my arms.

"You did! Was it fun?" He flew in his grandfather's jet quite a bit.

"Yeah," he said, nodding. Then his eyes lit up as he spotted Grant. "Dare's Until Gwant," he said, pointing. "See me, Until Gwant!" he called out. Grant turned his attention toward Nate's voice, and a grin spread across his face. Grant made his way over to us.

"Hey, bud!" he said, holding his fist out, which Nate hit with his own fist. The fact that Rush had taught his two-year-old to fist-bump was too funny. He also wore his baseball caps backward and drew pictures on his arms with a black marker whenever his mother wasn't watching. He wanted "pictures" on him like his daddy.

"See, my Betty," Nate said, patting my chest.

Grant chuckled. "Yeah, I see your Bethy. Did you fly in with Papa Dean?"

Nate nodded his head. "We flew da pwayne."

"I bet you did," Grant said.

"See Wywa Kate," Nate said, wiggling in my arms as Harlow walked in holding Lila Kate in her arms.

I took the hint and set Nate down. His little feet took off running toward Harlow and the baby.

"I think he may love your little girl more than me these days," I told Grant.

"Don't let it get to you. She's hard to compete with," Grant said with a grin. "I need to help Harlow with the wild man," he said before chasing after Nate. I watched as Grant caught up with Nate and scooped him up in his arms so he could see Lila Kate.

Nate was a charmer, and he'd make the complete rounds of the room before he remembered I was here and came back to see me. He loved to play the crowd.

I walked over to the tables, looking for my name. Everyone was coming in from the rehearsal and finding a seat. Walking down the aisle on Tripp's arm had been strange, but it hadn't been uncomfortable. He'd made a joke about me stumbling and taking him down with me. Other than that, we didn't really talk.

I sat down and looked over to see Thad's name on my right

and Blaire's name on my left. That meant Rush and Nate would also be at our table. And possibly Dean Finlay. Once that had been all the excitement I needed. But during the past two years, I'd managed to get over my starstruck behavior around Dean. Now he was just Rush's dad.

I wasn't sure who the last two seats were for. I pulled my chair out just as the chair beside mine moved. Expecting to see Thad, I saw Tripp instead. He smirked and sat down.

I cautiously did the same. Thad was supposed to be sitting there, but at the moment, he was nowhere to be found. If Tripp wanted to be friendly, I could do that. At least for one weekend, while we celebrated the marriage of our friends. When we got back to Rosemary Beach, I would need some boundaries. Seeing Tripp still reminded me of things I wanted to forget. I needed to take things slowly.

"You OK if I sit here?"

I glanced down at the place card and shrugged. "I don't mind, but Thad might. It's his assigned seat."

"Not worried about Thad. He's easy to bribe."

I turned to look at our friends gathering in the large ballroom. The stage crew was setting up for the band. I hadn't asked who was playing, but considering who was attending this wedding, I doubted it was just some cover band. With two of the members of Slacker Demon's kids in the wedding party and the drummer from Slacker Demon showing his grandson how to properly hold the drumsticks that Nate had snatched from the stage, the band was very likely to be a big name.

Woods and Della walked in, and everyone cheered as if they'd already gotten married, hooting and whistling. Clapping, I stood up and watched as they made their way to the center table. Della's smile lit up the room. Woods bent his head to whisper something in her ear, which made her blush. I could only imagine what he'd said to her.

Woods's eyes scanned the crowd and landed on Tripp. A frown creased his forehead. Woods and Della would have placed Tripp and Braden at their table, since they were the best man and the maid of honor. Woods nodded his head toward his table as he subtly signaled Tripp to move over there.

I glanced back at Tripp to make sure he saw Woods. "I think the best man is being summoned," I told him.

Tripp had a similar frown directed at Woods. "Yeah, I see that. I'll be right back," he said as he walked over to the bridal table.

Seeing Tripp standing by Woods at the rehearsal had been somewhat difficult. That would have been Jace standing there. Woods and Jace had been best friends since childhood. But Jace was gone, and Tripp was his stand-in. He symbolized the cousin who couldn't be here.

"An Betty!" called a familiar voice. I looked down just as Nate ran up to me and clambered into the chair beside me. "I sit by you," he informed me matter-of-factly.

"It's the only way we could get him to give the drummer his sticks back," Blaire said with an exasperated look.

"I got the bastard the gig. Least he could do was give my boy the damn sticks," Dean Finlay complained as he sauntered up to the table beside Rush.

"He tried to give him his extras," Blaire told Dean. I was beginning to think her exasperation came from dealing with her father-in-law and not her toddler.

"Stingy fucker," Dean muttered, pulling out the chair on the other side of Rush.

"Yeah, futter." Nate mimicked his grandfather. Blaire looked horrified.

"Dad. Language," Rush warned, then leaned over his wife and snapped his fingers at Nate to get his attention. "Remember what I told you about Papa's words. Mommy gets upset when you say them. We don't like upsetting Mommy, do we?"

Nate looked guilty and shook his head no.

"Apologize to Mommy and Aunt Bethy. Men don't say those words around ladies," Rush instructed him.

I had to bite back a smile. I'd heard Rush Finlay say a lot worse around women in my life. Hearing him tell his son not to was just too funny.

"I sowwy, Mommy," Nate mumbled, looking truly upset. Then he turned his daddy's silver eyes to me and repeated his apology.

"I didn't raise you to be a pus—"

"Dad." Rush cut his father off before he could finish his sentence. "You're upsetting Blaire. Stop it."

Dean chuckled and leaned back in his chair with an amused expression. "Good thing I like the pretty girl you married. I'll be good for her."

Rush leaned over to say something to Blaire, and she squeezed his arm to assure him that she was fine.

She looked at me and sighed heavily, then let out a soft laugh. "Life with a rock star as your kid's grandfather. Always interesting."

The chair beside me was pulled out, and I turned, expecting to see Tripp, but Thad's perfect white smile flashed at me. "What's up?" he said, giving us all a nod. "There's some really nice servers around this place," he said as he scooted his chair in. The lipstick mark on his neck made me giggle. I reached for a napkin.

"I can see that. She left some of her friendliness on your neck in candy-apple red. Come here."

A crooked grin tugged at his lips as he leaned over so I could wipe his neck clean. "You should see the friendliness I left on her," he whispered. At least he was observant of Nate's little ears.

"Was it the blonde or the brunette with the tight curls and big ti—"

"Dad!" Rush snarled, stopping Dean before he could finish that sentence, too.

Thad's grin only got bigger. "The blonde," he clarified.

Dean gave him a smirk. "Try the brunette next. She leaves her friendliness in much better places."

Gross. So not what I wanted to know.

"I swear to God, if you don't shut the hell up, I'm going to throw your old ass out of here," Rush warned his father.

Dean laughed and gave a shrug that had this badass rocker casualness to it. "Easy, boy," he told Rush, and patted his leg.

"OK, you two. Let's have fun," Blaire told them as Nate climbed into her lap.

Unable to help myself, I glanced over at the table Tripp was now seated at. He was talking to some female sitting beside him whom I didn't know. She hadn't been at the rehearsal, and she wasn't in the wedding party. The woman laughed at something Tripp said, and something in my stomach tightened up.

I would not acknowledge the feeling. I had no reason to care that Tripp was making some woman laugh. Even if she had really fabulous hair. It was golden and hung in long waves down her back. Who was she?

"Guess you haven't met Braden's cousin Charity," Blaire said, snapping me out of my obvious staring.

"No, I haven't," I said, forcing a smile.

"Charity just went through an ugly divorce last year, and Braden wanted to bring her to get her away from things. Thad and you were matched up for the dinners and the wedding. To make things even, Della thought it would be nice to have someone for Tripp so he wasn't the odd one out."

A wedding date. Della had supplied Tripp with a wedding date. That wasn't my business. I didn't care. Really. I didn't.

"Sweet," Thad said, putting his arm on the back of my chair and leaning back as he rested his ankle on his knee. "Bethy's my wedding date. Why didn't someone tell me? I'd never have run off with the blonde."

Rolling my eyes, I glanced back at Thad. "Because I'm not that friendly."

He nodded. "True, but I figure I can get a few drinks in you and loosen you up."

He was teasing me. I shook my head and reached for the glass of champagne that had been placed in front of me. "There isn't enough alcohol in the world, Thad," I informed him.

He slapped a hand over his heart. "Ouch. That's painful."

Taking a sip, I took one last glance at Tripp and Charity. Their heads were closer together now as they chatted away.

Awesome.

Tripp

This was not how I'd foreseen my night going. I couldn't believe Della had provided a date for the weekend. Why would she think I wanted that? Did I look like I needed a fucking date? Hell no.

Charity was attractive. I'd give Della that much—she had good taste. But I wasn't looking. I listened as Charity told me about the golden retriever puppy she'd just bought getting kicked out of doggy school for trying to hump a poodle. She laughed as she told me the story. If I weren't in love with Bethy, I'd be totally into her. She had a good laugh. Her brown eyes danced with amusement.

Woods had forced me to sit when I'd tried to tell him I was switching with Thad. He'd whispered in my ear what I already knew about Charity. "She's Braden's cousin, and she's had a bad divorce. She needs some attention. Do this for Della." His tone meant it wasn't a request.

I had sat reluctantly, glancing back at Bethy, who was once again being entertained by Nate. The kid knew a good-looking woman when he saw one. Thad's sorry ass would get to be with Bethy tonight. He'd get to talk to her. Hear her laugh.

He'd tell her stupid jokes that I knew she'd be amused by. Thad was good at charming females.

Damn player.

With his stupid pretty-boy looks.

I should have broken his nose years ago and evened the playing field. If I saw him touch Bethy tonight, I'd do more than break his nose.

I took a quick peek and saw Bethy listening to Dean Finlay. She seemed amused. At least it was the old man making her smile. Not Thad. Wait . . . No. Dean Finlay slept with women younger than me all the time. Maybe this wasn't good. He was a fucking rock god. Shit.

"Stop looking at Bethy like she's your last meal, dammit," Woods growled in a low voice beside me.

I turned my attention back to my table and glared at him. He met my angry glare with his own. Della cleared her throat loudly enough to get the attention of both of us. I let Woods deal with his woman as I reached for my drink. I needed something more than pink fucking bubbles.

"Do you surf, too?" Charity asked beside me.

Were we talking about surfing now? Shit, I didn't know. I was so checked out of this conversation. Focusing was an issue, with Dean Finlay and Thad both flirting with Bethy.

"Uh, yeah. I mean, I did back in the day. I haven't in a while. We don't get the waves in the Gulf to make it really worth it."

"Didn't you live in Myrtle Beach for a while?" she asked.

Had I told her that? "Yeah, I did. It was short-lived," I replied.

I looked over at Della, who was watching me with her bottom lip between her teeth. She was concerned. I knew that look.

I'd spent a lot of time with Della back when she and Woods were figuring things out. When you spend two solid weeks on the road with someone, you get to know each other well.

I was being selfish. This was her wedding weekend, and I was worried about me. I forced myself to relax and turned my attention back to Charity. I could do this. Bethy wasn't going to hook up with Thad or Dean. I knew better than that. My stupid jealousy was rattling my brain.

"Why? Do you surf?" I asked Charity, hoping she hadn't already said she did.

She laughed and shook her head. "No. I'm extremely un-coordinated. But if you wanted to give me lessons, I wouldn't turn them down."

Oh, hell. I'd walked right into that one. I cut my eyes at Della, who was listening with a nervous expression. "Sure. I can do that if you want," I agreed, hoping I never saw her again after we left the island on Sunday.

Charity looked giddy with delight. "Yes, I'd love to!"

"Good idea. Why don't you take her out in the morning for a lesson?" Woods said.

I opened my mouth to spout some bullshit excuse for why that wasn't happening. But Charity clapped her hands and beamed at me. "Oh, how exciting!"

Well, shit.

❖

I danced with Charity twice before I was able to extract myself to find Bethy, but she wasn't at her table or on the dance floor. Scanning the crowd and tables, I didn't see her anywhere. Then I looked for Thad and realized he was missing, too.

What the hell?

I started moving for the door. I wasn't explaining my exit to Woods. He'd do something else to screw it up. I had done my job all during dinner, and then I'd danced with Charity. Not to mention that I had to take her surfing in the morning. I was done with my goodwill for the evening.

I stalked out of the building and across the sand, keeping my eyes open for a sign of Bethy.

A giggle stopped me, and I turned to walk around the building and into a small thicket of palm trees.

"Got a famous mouth, now, don't you," Thad teased, and I tensed up. I followed the rumble of his voice as he made a groan. "Fuck, yes, take it all the way in. Back of your throat, baby," he encouraged.

I stopped. There was no fucking way that was Bethy. She wouldn't be sucking him off. The clouds shifted, and the moon lit up my surroundings. Thad's eyes lifted from the girl knelt between his legs to meet mine.

He put his finger over his mouth to silence me. He didn't want an interruption. The girl had brown curly hair and had on one of the uniforms the servers were wearing. It wasn't Bethy. Thank fuck.

I turned and walked back toward the path leading to our huts.

"Oh, shit! Swallow the head. Yeah, God, yes!" Thad cried out.

I walked faster. I didn't want to hear him get off. But if he didn't keep it down, the whole damn island was going to hear him.

Bethy

I slipped my heels off and walked back out to curl up on the lounger and look out over the water. After watching Tripp dance with Charity for half a song, I'd realized I really needed to leave. It bothered me. Not that I should be surprised. I had been jealous of Della, too, back when I thought Tripp had a thing for her. I'd had Jace then, and I had no right to be jealous, but with Tripp, I didn't seem to have control over my emotions.

Which sucked.

Being friends with him was my way of calling a truce. Finding a common ground so I could focus on living again instead of living with so much guilt and hate. Watching Tripp with other women, however, wasn't part of the deal. Once this weekend was over, I would smile at Tripp when I saw him and keep it casual. No reason to be close friends.

Although I wondered if this meant he wouldn't follow me to and from work anymore. Would I miss him sitting outside my apartment staring at my window for hours?

Yes.

That sucked, too. As much as I told myself I hated him for following me and sitting outside my apartment, the truth was, I was mad at myself for wanting it. For expecting it.

All these frustrated emotions weren't things I'd had to deal with in my relationship with Jace. I'd been secure and safe. The drama and pent-up emotions I always experienced with Tripp had never been there with Jace. It had just been easier.

So what if Tripp was with Charity tonight? It wasn't like I was ever going to be more than his friend. Seeing him made my heart speed up, and when he smiled, my stomach did a little fluttery thing. It always had. But that wasn't enough. With Tripp came so much pain. I didn't want that pain. I was closing the door on it and moving on.

"You checked out early." Tripp's voice startled me, and I jumped. "Sorry. Didn't mean to scare you," he said, smiling at my reaction.

He didn't need to be here right now. Why wasn't he with the blonde? Far away from me and my screwed-up thoughts. "It's been a long day," I replied simply.

His hands were in his pockets, and he had unbuttoned the top of his white shirt and rolled up the sleeves, revealing a peep of the tattoos that colored his arms. He stood with his legs slightly apart as he studied me. He was so dang tall.

"Want company?" he asked, looking at the space beside me. No. Yes. Crap.

I shrugged instead of answering, since I didn't have a definite answer.

He took that as an affirmative and sat down on the lounger. There was enough space for two, but it was a small space, which meant his long legs stretched out in front of him and touched mine. He crossed them at the ankles and leaned back.

"It's peaceful here," he said in a reverent tone.

I nodded. I wasn't much for talking. Until yesterday, I had

him in my "hate you" box. It had been all I allowed myself to feel where he was concerned. Now that I had taken him out, I didn't know where to put him. Preferably in a box that didn't allow me to care that he was with other females.

"Not now, because I realize I'm on really fragile ground with you, but one day, when you're ready, I want a chance to explain what happened eight years ago."

Not what I had expected him to say. I thought we were going to pretend that didn't happen and move on with our lives. "What's past is past. Let's leave it where it belongs," I said, not looking at him. My hands fisted firmly in my lap as a wave of emotions washed over me at once. The heartache, loss, fear, and intense love I'd pushed away. I didn't want it.

"I'd agree with you if you actually knew the past. But you don't. Just like there are things I don't know. Things I want to know, even if it's going to rip me open. I need to know, Bethy. For us both to find a way to heal, we have to deal with the past first."

He was right. But I wasn't ready. Our past was what would define the rest of my life. He had molded me into who I was. Our relationship had been the source of my greatest regrets and mistakes. "I'm not ready," I said quietly.

He didn't reply, and I almost expected him to get up and leave. But after a few moments, his hand moved over and covered mine. The warmth and size of it engulfed my hand, and I would be a liar if I said it wasn't comforting. With that one small gesture, I was reminded that I wasn't alone in this. He understood more than anyone else what I was dealing with.

The night grew darker, and the silence wrapped around us like a cocoon. A place where the past seemed distant and the future was unknown.

Tripp

Teaching a woman how to surf, when she was making it very clear that she wanted me in her bed, was uncomfortable. I knew I had my hands full with each flirty remark that came out of Charity's mouth. The fact she'd been through a bad divorce and needed male attention made me feel sorry for her. But that didn't mean I was going to be the guy to give her that attention. Not after Bethy had let me sit with her for more than an hour last night and hold her hand. We hadn't talked much, but just being there with her had been enough for me. It was progress.

Charity giggled at her last attempt to crawl onto the board, then turned to me and batted her eyelashes. "Help," she said.

That was another thing. She kept wanting me to put her on the damn board, and she wasn't wearing much of a bikini. Too much skin contact.

"Try it by yourself this time," I instructed her, not wanting to grab her waist again. She shivered every time I touched her, and I felt guilty. I didn't want her thinking this was going anywhere. I wasn't her wedding fuck. Unfortunately, she hadn't figured that out yet.

"I like it better when you help me," she said, dropping her

voice down a notch to what I was sure would be a sexy sound to most men.

We had been at it for an hour. I'd done my duty. It was time to put an end to the ideas running through her head. "Yeah, well, I'm beat. We both have a wedding to get ready for this afternoon and a long night of celebrating ahead. Probably shouldn't overdo it."

With that excuse, I slipped the board under my arm and nodded for her to follow me before walking back to the shore.

"Oh, OK," she called out behind me, and hurried to catch up.

I didn't give her reason to think I wanted to prolong this; I just kept walking.

"Uh, so did you eat breakfast already?" she asked, catching up to me quickly.

I had only grabbed a cup of coffee before heading out, but eating with her wasn't happening, either. She was getting too bold. "Not a breakfast eater," I replied, which was a lie. After being out in the waves, I was starving.

"Oh, well, I guess I'll see you later?" she asked as we finally made it to shore.

I nodded. "Sure," I agreed, because I would. We'd both be at the wedding.

Then I headed up the small incline toward the other side of the island where the huts were located.

"You look like a man running from something," Woods said with an amused smirk as he stepped out from a cluster of palm trees with a cup of coffee in his hands.

I shot him a warning glare. "This shit isn't funny."

Woods chuckled and took a sip. "I don't know. Watching you dodge female advances is new. I was entertained."

"I'm putting up with this for Della. But if this causes me any issues with Bethy, it ends. Charity's nice, and I know she's been through a shitty time. I feel bad for her. But I'm making some headway with Bethy, and nothing is standing in my way of that."

Woods's smirk faded. He stared out at the water for a moment, and I knew his thoughts were with Jace. This should have been a day that Jace stood by his side. It should be Jace handing him the ring and giving a toast at the reception. Today Woods would start a new journey in life, and he would do it without his best friend there to cheer him on. It was all there in his eyes. "She seems better," he said.

After last night, I had to agree. Anger and pain were no longer boiling out of her. "Yeah. She does."

Woods took another drink of his coffee. "Don't push her. You weren't here for most of it, but she loved him. They were good together."

I already knew how much she had loved Jace. That hadn't been hard to miss. "I'm being careful. I don't want to take Jace's place. He's got that spot in her heart, and he always will. Right now, I just want to be there for her. To see her smile again. A real smile."

"He would have wanted her happy. And he would have beaten my ass for treating her the way I did. I doubt he would've forgiven me for what I said to her that night on the beach." His voice sounded pained.

I hadn't been there, but I knew from the silent treatment he'd given her for more than a year after Jace's death that he'd blamed her. He was right—Jace wouldn't have been able to forgive him for that. He'd loved Bethy. But that wasn't what

Woods needed to hear right now. This was supposed to be one of the happiest days of his life.

"He may have been my cousin, but you were like his brother. He loved you," I told him.

"I let him down," Woods said.

"No, you didn't. You saved her. That's what he asked you to do, and you did it."

Woods finally moved his gaze back to mine. I could see the emotion I understood so well. Jace had left an empty place in all of us.

"He died knowing that his best friend made a sacrifice for him that would mark him for the rest of his life. You were his hero."

Woods studied me for a moment and then turned his attention back to the water.

After a few moments of silence, I stepped around him and made my way toward the huts once again.

"Thanks," Woods called out. I glanced back at him. "I needed to hear that. Especially today."

I managed a smile. "That's what a best man is for," I replied, and left him there with his thoughts.

Bethy

*T*ripp trailed soft kisses up and down my body while he held himself rigid above me. The pain from his entrance had taken my breath away, but he had stopped the second I cried out. He hadn't pulled out, which was all I wanted him to do, so I could curl up in a ball and whimper.

But then he'd started kissing me gently and whispering in my ear.

"It's OK. I won't move. Just let me feel you. God, Bethy, nothing has ever felt like this."

Hearing the pleasure in his voice as he kissed me, as if he couldn't get enough of me, eased the tension. Slowly, he sank deeper, until he let out a loud groan and closed his eyes. He was beautiful, and I was completely fascinated.

"I'm going to move," he said against my ear, and then he sucked in a sharp breath as he pulled back until he was almost out of me and then rocked his hips back.

The movement hadn't caused me pain this time, at least not the searing kind it had the first time. Just a little discomfort. Watching Tripp made everything else fade away. The veins in his neck were standing out, and the muscles in his arms were bulging as he held himself up so that he didn't put all his weight on me.

With each move of his hips, it got easier, and Tripp's face became more breathtaking. His mouth opened slightly, and his pupils were so dilated the green was almost gone.

Our gazes locked.

"I love you. I won't leave you. I can't."

My eyes opened, and I stared at the ceiling. I hadn't dreamed about that night in a very long time. My heart was racing, as if I was still there underneath him, losing my virginity to the boy I loved and hearing him proclaim his love for me for the first time. He'd made a lot of promises that night that he didn't keep.

I sat up and shook my head, not wanting that image to replay in my mind. I had pushed it away a long time ago. I had used other guys in hopes of washing it from my memory. But no one ever did. It always ended with me crying myself to sleep.

Last night, I had let Tripp get close again. Even though we hadn't spoken, I had allowed him to sit with me, releasing long-suppressed emotions and images. No wonder my dreams played out more like memories.

Getting up, I grabbed my black silk wrap and put it on before raising the walls around my hut. I didn't want to leave until it was time to help Della get ready. She had said we would meet in the bride's room at one. I would have breakfast brought to me and enjoy my solitude until then.

"Hungry?" Tripp asked. I spun around to see him holding a tray of food.

With the memory of our first time still fresh in my head, I did *not* need this right now. My eyes, however, had other ideas. His arms were bigger now. Thicker than they had been before.

His hair was shorter and looked damp, as if he'd just stepped out of the shower, although the board shorts suggested that he might have been swimming. Then there was the fact that he was shirtless. All those defined muscles, tanned and decorated with a few well-placed tattoos, would make any woman stop and stare.

"I was going to eat outside of my place, but you opened yours before I could sit down. I figured I had enough to share," he said, snapping me out of my momentary lack of good sense.

I jerked my eyes back up to meet his. I had to hand it to him—he didn't look smug, even though I knew he noticed I had just given him a once-over. He was being careful. "I, uh, OK," I managed to stammer out.

He grinned and stepped inside, then placed the tray on the round high-top table, which had two bar stools underneath it. "I'll even let you have the eggs," he said, as if he needed to sweeten the deal so I wouldn't change my mind.

His arms didn't have to be flexed for his muscles to stand out. They did that all on their own now. I could even see veins in them as he went about fixing us both a cup of coffee and setting out all three plates of food he'd brought with him.

He needed to put a shirt on, dammit. How was I supposed to eat and not stare at that?

God, Bethy, nothing has ever felt like this.

I closed my eyes tightly and blocked out Tripp's words replaying in my head.

"You OK?" he asked in his older, more mature voice. I managed a nod and opened my eyes.

"Sun's a little bright. My eyes are adjusting," I lied.

Tripp frowned and walked over to adjust the shade. "Better?" he asked.

"Mmm-hmm," I replied, hoping my guilty thoughts weren't all over my face.

He walked back over to the table and pulled out a bar stool, then motioned for me to take it. I mumbled a thank you and climbed up. My wrap rode up my thighs and fell open, revealing almost all of my legs. I grabbed the edges to pull them together but not before Tripp noticed. My breathing hitched as I watched his eyes lock on my thighs. His nostrils flared, and his entire body tensed.

If the veins on his neck popped out, I was done for. I had to get control of things. Grabbing the edges, I tucked them around me. He tore his gaze off me and moved over to the other side of the table, faster than normal.

Clearing his throat, he slid a plate filled with eggs, fruit, some cheese, buttered toast, and a few slices of bacon toward me. "As promised, the eggs."

My face was warm from the many emotions whirling around in my head. In an attempt to make things less awkward, I smiled at him. "Thank you. But I don't need all the eggs. I can share."

He shrugged. "I'm good. You eat what you want, and I'll finish off what you don't eat."

Like we used to do.

Ugh. Why was I doing this? He hadn't meant that. He was just referring to the eggs. He wasn't trying to remind me of how things had been once. That was all me. Stupid dream had me all hot and bothered.

"OK," I replied, hoping my reaction appeared normal.

He took a bite of his toast. As his jaw moved, the muscles in his neck flexed. Shit! What was wrong with me?

I dropped my gaze and grabbed something off my plate. I didn't even care what. Luckily, it was a strawberry. I popped it into my mouth and began to chew.

We ate in silence for a few minutes. I wasn't sure what to say and hated that it was just getting more awkward. But every time I looked at him, I saw my dream replaying again in my head.

"Is everything OK? I just thought you might want to eat. If you want me to, I can take my plate and go next door." Tripp's eyes were on me, and I had to meet his gaze to respond.

I started to say that it was OK but realized that wasn't the truth. Tripp knew me well enough to know I was lying. If we were going to be friends again, or at least attempt it, then I had to be honest with him. Well, not completely honest. I didn't want him knowing I'd dreamed about our first time in extreme detail. "This is going to take some adjustment," I said as I finally met his gaze. "I want to move on from everything. Like we discussed. But I'm not sure how. I'm trying to figure it out."

Tripp pulled his bottom lip through his teeth as a frown creased his brow. He didn't need to bite his lip; that was taking an unfair advantage. He had to know that was sexy. I didn't need sexy Tripp faces. "Fair enough," he replied. Then a naughty grin touched his lips, and he dropped his eyes from mine to look at the table. "Maybe next time, I'll give you a sec to put on something other than a little silky piece of fabric."

He was teasing me. Friendly teasing. I could do this. "Maybe next time, you could wear a shirt," I countered.

His gaze shot back up to mine, and for a second, I wasn't sure if I should have said that. I might have given him the wrong idea. But then he surprised me and laughed. The deep chuckle that used to set butterflies off in my stomach and make me light-headed.

And it still did.

"Fair enough. We'll dress more appropriately next time."

I nodded as a smile settled on my lips. I relaxed and reached for my fork so I could eat my eggs.

Tripp

Keeping my focus on Woods and Della during the ceremony was difficult. The pale blue dress Bethy was wearing clung to her curves, which proved extremely distracting. I had the ring, and I didn't want to miss my cue, but damn, it was hard not to watch Bethy.

The loose curls that hadn't been pulled up on her head brushed her face as they got caught in the breeze. I wanted to walk over and pull out whatever was holding her hair up and watch it all fall down in a tangle of curls. I had never seen her hair curled before, and although I liked it just fine when it was straight, I wanted to wrap those curls around my fingers.

"You became my safe place after you stole my heart." Della's words brought me out of my Bethy fog. That was my cue. I slipped my hand into my pocket and pulled out the ring, then handed it to Woods. It was his turn to say the vows he'd written for her.

Grant had tried to get him to rehearse them earlier in front of us, but he wouldn't. He'd said he didn't need to rehearse. He didn't even have a cheat sheet to give me in case he needed any help.

"My life lacked purpose and meaning. I was going through the motions, unaware that I was hollow inside. Then one night, this gorgeous brunette lit up the bleakness within me. She was only in town for a night, but luckily, fate gave me a second chance and placed her in my path one more time.

"You changed everything for me, Della. When you're beside me, I can do anything. I can face any challenge and walk through any fire. As long as you're the one holding my hand. You tell me I'm your safe place, but you have more strength and courage than anyone I've ever known.

"No one will ever come before you. I'll spend forever making sure you always feel safe. Never doubt for a second that you own my heart. You're my life."

Della's sob was followed by several others. My gaze moved back to Bethy, and I watched as she wiped away her own tears. Fate had given Woods another chance. I sure as hell hoped fate gave me one, too.

The crowd roared, and I turned back to see Woods dip Della back as he held her in his arms and kissed her. When he was finally done making out with his wife in public, he took her arm, and they walked back down the aisle as Mr. and Mrs. Woods Kerrington.

Thad stepped forward from behind me and took Braden's arm as they followed the couple out. I waited for Bethy's move. When she walked forward, I met her in the middle of the aisle and held out my arm for her to take. She slipped hers through mine, and I tucked it close to my body. It wasn't the way the drill sergeant had told us to do it, but I didn't give a shit. I'd just spent the last thirty minutes wanting to touch Bethy and not being able to. This was my excuse to get close to her, and I was taking it. She didn't fight me; she let me keep her against me as we followed the others.

"You smell good," I said as I bent my head down to inhale her sweet perfume.

She tensed but only for a moment. "Thank you," she whispered.

I watched as Thad dropped his arm and Braden moved forward, looking around for her husband with a bright smile on her face. We were all supposed to go to the large tent set up for the reception in the center of the island. But unless Bethy pulled away from me, I wasn't letting go.

Woods had stopped up ahead and was cradling Della's face in his hands and kissing her. Again.

"Damn, man. Stop sucking her face off. You got the rest of your life for that. Let's go party!" Thad called out.

Woods ignored him.

"I'm so happy for them," Bethy said.

I was, too. "Yeah," I agreed.

"Honeymoon starts after the reception. Brides are funny about that shit!" Rush called out.

This time, Della broke the kiss and looked back at us with laughter in her eyes. "You're right. I want to dance with my husband," she said.

The look of possessiveness on Woods's face as she called him her husband didn't go unnoticed by anyone.

"Wait until she realizes what happens every time she refers to him as her husband," Blaire said as she and Rush stopped beside us.

Bethy laughed, but it wasn't a full laugh. There was a sad-

YOU WERE MINE 125

ness there. I fucking hated that. I didn't want her sad. She'd been sad for so long.

"Let's go party," I said, stopping the blissful married sex talk and tightening my hold on Bethy as I led her toward the reception.

Once we reached the tent, Bethy pulled away and gave me a small, embarrassed smile. She hadn't realized I was still holding on to her until that moment—it was obvious from the look on her face. She'd been comfortable with me holding her, and damn, I liked that. "You'll be at the bride and groom's table over there." She pointed to the table closest to the dance floor, with the most elaborate centerpiece.

I hadn't realized I wouldn't be able to sit by her again. Did this mean I had to sit next to Charity? Shit.

"We're here, Bethy," Blaire called out to her from across the dance floor. They were also close to the dance floor but on the other side of the room.

"Enjoy the dinner," she said before turning and walking away from me. I watched as her hips swayed and her satin dress moved over her ass. God, she was gorgeous. But then, she always had been.

"I believe you're my dinner partner again tonight," an unwelcomed female voice said, interrupting my thoughts.

I glanced over at Charity. She was beaming a little too brightly. Almost as if she was forcing her joy. This probably hadn't been easy on her, either. She'd thought she would have a happily-ever-after once, too. It hadn't turned out that way.

"Yeah, I'm sure we are," I replied with a halfhearted smile, and motioned for her to lead the way.

Bethy

The tinkling sound of the spoon hitting the champagne glass quieted the room, and I turned around, knowing who had caught everyone's attention. It was time for the maid of honor and the best man to make their speeches. I had tried to keep my eyes off that table since I sat down. I wasn't a fan of the beautiful blonde, Charity.

Was I jealous?

Yes. Yes, I was.

Tripp grinned, and I was sure every single female guest melted a little. "It appears I'm going first," he said, then cocked a teasing eyebrow at Braden. Laughter filled the tent.

"First of all, I'd like to take all the credit for this," he said, waving a hand at Woods and Della. "I was the one who sent Della to Rosemary Beach, or back to Rosemary Beach. I had no idea she'd passed through months earlier. But regardless, she came back because of me."

More laughter. It was no surprise Tripp was good at this. He had always been able to charm a crowd.

"I didn't realize the infamous Woods Kerrington was in deep until the night he walked into my apartment for my welcome-home party. It's a wonder I'm standing here today.

The man had staked his claim, and he was prepared to take down anyone in his way." He paused again while everyone laughed. They all knew exactly what he was referring to.

"Della's special. I knew it the moment I met her. But I could see in her eyes the same lost soul I saw in my own mirror every day. We were kindred spirits. All I knew was that if I could go back to Rosemary Beach, then maybe I'd have a chance of finding myself. But I wasn't ready. So I did the next best thing. I sent Della. If I wasn't ready to help myself, I wanted to at least help her." He stopped and looked down at Woods. "And I was right. When I look at Della now, that lost look is completely gone. There's joy and love shining in her eyes.

"And you." He nudged Woods. "Dude, you're so completely owned." Laughter rang out, and Della leaned into her husband, holding his arm tightly.

"Once you asked me to hold her because you couldn't. You didn't want her to be alone. But what I understood then, which you hadn't quite figured out yet, was that you're the only one who can hold her, man. Your arms are her home."

Tripp looked back out at the crowd and held up his champagne glass. "I'd wish you all the happiness in the world, but you've both already got that. Congratulations, you two. Cheers."

I took a sip of my champagne and watched as Della stood up and threw her arms around Tripp, happy tears shining in her eyes. Woods stood up and casually took his wife's arm and made a show of bringing her possessively to his side. Then he shook Tripp's hand and thanked him before leaning in and saying something in his ear and slapping him on the back.

Grinning, both men sat down.

"I would hate to be Braden and have to follow that up. He was fantastic," Blaire whispered.

I completely agreed with her.

⊞

Thad was a good dance partner, but his eyes were on a pretty server who also had her eyes on him. As soon as the dance was finished, I leaned in close to his ear. "Make sure you don't get caught. She'll probably get fired," I warned him.

He winked at me. "I'm always careful."

I laughed and walked back to our table. Dean was sitting there with Nate, and they had taken the spoons from the table and were using them as drumsticks. Nate was listening carefully to his grandfather's explanations about how to keep the beat.

Rush and Blaire were still on the dance floor. I watched Della as she danced with her father. A man she had never known existed until two years ago. When Della had first come to Rosemary Beach, she had no family, just her best friend, Braden, and a lot of screwed-up shit in her past.

"I pway the dwums, An Betty," Nate informed me loudly over the music.

"I see that. You sound great!" I assured him.

He beamed the charming little smile he'd inherited from his father at me. Then he went back to beating on the table with his spoons. Surprisingly in rhythm to the music. Maybe the kid had gotten his grandfather's musical talent.

"Dance with me?" Tripp asked just before he stepped in front of me.

It was ridiculously unfair for this man to be in a tuxedo. There had to be a law against it. All six-foot-five of him looked more like the wealthy, elite man he could have been instead of the rebel on a bike he'd become.

He had been entertaining Braden's cousin all evening. I had forbidden myself to look over at them after my stomach got knotted up so badly I could hardly eat. I wasn't going to do this to myself. "Don't you need to dance with your date?" I asked, unable to keep the cattiness from my voice. It wasn't his fault Della had brought him a wedding date. I would not think about the wedding sex I was sure the woman was expecting.

"I've already danced with her. Now I want to dance with you."

And I wasn't sure I could keep from pawing at him in his damn suit if he put his arms around me. Why did this man have to look like this? Why couldn't he have gotten ugly with age?

"Please, Bethy." His voice had lowered.

Like I could tell him no. I slipped my hand into his outstretched one and stood up.

"Smart girl," Dean said.

I swung my gaze over to him. He winked at me and gave Tripp a thumbs-up before going back to the drum lesson with Nate.

"It's OK. It's just a dance," Tripp said, pulling my hand until I was close to him and farther away from the table.

Dean's comments weren't why I couldn't relax. It was the idea of being in Tripp's arms.

We walked out onto the floor just as the music slowed and James Morrison began singing "I Won't Let You Go."

One of Tripp's hands found my lower back as he put gentle pressure on me to move closer while his other hand rested on my hip. I was thankful I had on six-inch stilettos so I could rest my hands on his shoulders.

"You can do better than that," Tripp whispered in my ear. My traitorous body shivered.

"What?" I asked.

His hands left me and reached up to take mine and place them around his neck before going back to my lower back and hip. "Much better," he said as our bodies brushed against each other.

This was close. Too close.

"You smell incredible," he whispered, pressing me even closer.

OK, too much. The warmth of his body was surrounding me, and I was getting light-headed. Maybe because I was forgetting to breathe. When I breathed in, the clean scent of his soap washed over me. He rarely wore cologne. He either smelled like the sea breeze from riding his bike or like this. Either way, I used to love pulling him close and inhaling.

"You look beautiful tonight. I almost felt sorry for the other bridesmaids having to wear the same dress as you."

If anyone else had said that, I would have laughed and rolled my eyes. Blaire Finlay was the closest thing I had seen to perfection in my life. And Harlow Carter had the classic kind of beauty you don't see often. But hearing Tripp say it, I believed him.

I touched the collar of his tux and rubbed the expensive fabric between my fingers. This wasn't a rented tux. It was probably Armani. None of these guys needed a rented tux. It had been a part of their wardrobe since they were kids. Their lifestyles often required a tuxedo.

"You do tuxes well. I've never seen you in one," I replied finally. It was the closest thing I could say to the truth. Telling him it made my heart race in my chest was a bad idea.

He chuckled. "Thanks. I'm not a fan. It's been a while since I've had to wear one. This one is new. I figured if I was staying in Rosemary Beach, I'd need to add a few pieces to my wardrobe."

He was staying in Rosemary Beach? Why? Because he wanted to be home? "You won't miss the open road and being able to pick up and take off whenever you want?" I asked, thinking about what I knew of his life since he'd left.

The next song began, and he pulled me closer. "I'm done running, and there's nothing for me out there. What I want is in Rosemary Beach."

He didn't mean me. Not me. I didn't want him to mean me. The romantic world we were wrapped in on this island was fleeting. Tomorrow we faced reality again. And, with it, the past.

I didn't respond to him. Those weren't words I wanted to say out loud right now. I wanted this fantasy for tonight. The fairy tale that I could be here, wrapped up in Tripp's arms forever. We could dance like this, and I could feel his heartbeat and watch the pulse beating at the base of his throat. The warmth of his embrace was mine to keep. In this moment, I could pretend.

Tripp

I wasn't being careful. Having her in my arms was making shit come out of my mouth that was going to fuck up the progress we'd made. I clenched my jaw tightly to keep from telling her how good she felt—and exactly what I wanted to do to her while she wore nothing but those sexy-ass heels.

I bent my head and inhaled deeply. If I could just press my lips to that curve in her neck. Maybe take a soft taste of her skin with the flick of my tongue. She used to make the sweetest sounds when I did that. Her body wasn't tensed up anymore. She had her arms wrapped around me and her chest pressed against mine. The feeling of her leaning into me was heady.

Lifting my eyes from the soft skin so close to my mouth, I saw Woods glaring at me. What was his deal? He needed to dance with his wife and let me have this. He nodded his head to the left, and I looked over to see Charity sitting at the table alone. Oh, hell no. He wasn't going to make me feel bad about that. Shit. Shit!

I looked back at him, and he gave another sharp nod of his head. I saw Della walking over to her. Well, fuck. Della wasn't enjoying her own party because she was worrying about

Charity. This seriously sucked. I was going to have to go over there so Della could go back to enjoying herself.

Where was Braden? It was her cousin, dammit. Why wasn't she entertaining her cousin? I didn't ask for a damn date. If I'd wanted a date, I'd have brought one.

Bethy's fingers slipped into the hair at the back of my neck. Oh, fuck. I closed my eyes as she began running her nails up my neck softly. How was I supposed to walk away from this? God, I was in heaven.

My hand slipped lower down her back until the curve of her ass was under my fingertips. She didn't move away, and I wasn't breathing anymore. Tearing my eyes open before I completely lost myself, I saw that Woods was now walking toward me. He looked determined.

I was ready to plead with him to leave me the hell alone. Let me have this. He had no idea what eight years felt like. He'd had to go without Della for only two damn weeks before. He needed to try eight motherfucking years.

Thad walked by, and Woods grabbed his arm and said something to him. Thad's gaze swung to me. He looked apologetic as he nodded his head. Woods was sending him over to cut in so I'd have to let her go.

Bethy chose that moment to run her nails down the front of my chest and stare up at me with those big brown eyes. I had to say something. Explain or apologize. Even though this shit was not my fault.

"Hey, dude. Share. You've had her for like the last five songs. My turn," Thad said in a teasing tone that didn't meet his eyes. He was watching me like I might take a swing at him.

Bethy blinked and seemed a little dazed and confused before she looked over at Thad, but her hands remained fixed on my body, and she didn't move back. I was real damn close to pounding my chest in a very caveman move.

"Seriously, Bethy. Dance with me. Tripp needs to give a little attention to his, uh . . . well, the lady sitting beside him."

"Oh," Bethy said as awareness of what was happening dawned on her. She looked at her hands, still on me, then dropped them quickly and stepped back. "Right," she said, glancing around nervously. "I'm sorry."

I'd go dance with the woman to make Woods happy, but I wasn't letting Bethy apologize. Fuck that. I grabbed her hand and tugged her back against me. "Do not apologize. Not for that," I said, and then I placed her hand in Thad's. "Careful," I warned under my voice as I walked past him.

I turned all my frustration toward Woods, who was watching. He at least looked somewhat sorry.

Walking up to the table, I heard Charity trying to get Della to go dance with her husband and not to worry about her. Why couldn't Thad have danced with her? Why did it have to be me? I shoved away the guilt that was trying to force its way through and put on a fake smile.

"Hey, Della, aren't you supposed to be dancing? It's your wedding," I reminded her.

Della looked up at me with relief in her eyes. "Oh, yes, I was just visiting with Charity. Braden wasn't feeling well. She's been on her feet too long today. This second pregnancy is kicking her butt."

Great. That answered my question from earlier. "I'll visit with Charity. You go dance with your husband. He looks lonely," I told her.

She smiled at me and nodded, then said good-bye to Charity before hurrying back to Woods. This was their night. I would do this for them. This once. But never again. And for no one else.

"You seemed very taken with the other dance partner you had. Did someone take her away from you?" Charity asked. I didn't miss the annoyed tone in her voice.

I had the warmth of Bethy still in my arms. I wasn't ready to have someone else replace that. I took a seat beside Charity instead of asking her to dance. "You enjoying yourself?" I asked, completely ignoring her comment.

She raised her eyebrows as if she was surprised I cared.

I was purposely not looking at Bethy in Thad's arms. I couldn't be sure I wouldn't storm back there and take her away from him.

"My date has been very wrapped up with another woman for the past half hour. What do you think?" Her retort was sharp this time.

I leaned forward and started to inform her that she wasn't my fucking date. She was here because Della invited her, not because I asked her. All I wanted right now was to go back out there and hold Bethy the only way she would let me. But I caught myself. I wasn't cruel. Charity was a scorned woman who had been burned by her husband. She was at a wedding with a bunch of happily married people. She was hurting. And I, as one of the few bachelors here, was an easy target. I got that. "I'm in love with her," I said. Charity needed to know that my attention was never going to be turned her way.

Charity rolled her eyes. "Sure you are. Big boobs and all those curves. I'm sure it's love, all right."

Reminding myself once again that Charity was going through a tough time was hard. "Yes, she's beautiful, but it's deeper than that," I said, unable to hide that she'd pissed me off.

"Men. You see something you think is easy, and you're all like panting dogs. News flash: tonight *I* was going to be easy."

My hands fisted as I leveled my furious glare on her. She'd stepped over the line. No one, fucking no one, referred to Bethy as easy. Leaning forward, I clenched my teeth so tightly my jaw popped.

Charity sat back as her eyes went wide with fear.

I didn't lose my shit often, but this woman was pushing me. "When I was eighteen years old, I fell in love. Not the first love kind of love but the big kind. The one-and-only kind of love. But because of parents who wanted to turn me into someone I wasn't, I had to run to save myself. She was only sixteen and I couldn't take her with me. When I ran, I did it for us, so I could come back for her when she was old enough." The hard edge to my voice made her shoulders jerk and her face pale, but she was listening.

"But that didn't happen. While I was running, she was facing something terrifying without me. I wasn't there to stand by her and hold her. Because of that, I lost her. Years later, she fell in love again. With my cousin. And he was the better man.

"When I finally came home to face my demons, she was happy. More than anything on this earth, I wanted her happy. But again, tragedy hit us. A riptide pulled my cousin under the water while he was trying to save her life, and we both lost him.

"For eighteen months, I've had to watch as the woman I love walked through life lost. Hollow from her loss. She wouldn't let me near her, because all I did was remind her of everything she'd lost. She yelled at me and said things that sliced me open in ways I don't think I'll ever recover from. But still, I follow her and watch over her every day. Because she's alone. And I have to know she's safe. It's the only thing that keeps me going." The angry tone in my voice was gone. I sounded as desperate as I felt.

Charity's expression softened, and the shock in her eyes was replaced with sympathy. I looked out onto the dance floor as Dean Finlay, who had taken over for Thad, twirled Bethy around, making her smile.

"Tonight, for the first time in eight very long years, she let me hold her. She didn't yell at me. She didn't push me away. My cousin's best friend got married tonight, and instead of my cousin standing up there as his best man, I had to take his place. But even with that reminder hovering over the night, she let me hold her."

Charity followed my gaze and then made a soft "oh" sound.

I wasn't sure why I told her everything. I wanted her to understand that I knew all about pain. She wasn't the only one with shit in her past. I also wanted her to get that I would not be sleeping with her tonight.

"That's her, then," Charity said, watching Bethy laugh at Dean's antics.

"Yeah, that's her."

"She's beautiful," Charity said in a whisper.

"The most beautiful woman I've ever seen."

She sniffed and wiped at her eyes. When I looked back at her, she smiled. "That's a heartbreaking story. But it makes me believe there's more out there for me. What I had was never that kind of love. I thought that kind of love was only in the movies. Seeing your face when you talk about her, that's what I want." She stood up, and her smile brightened. "Thank you. For telling me all that. I was sitting here feeling sorry for myself. I'll admit, I was angry at you for not giving me any attention. But after hearing that and watching Della and Woods together, I know that Braden and Adam aren't one of a kind. There really is someone out there for everyone. I've got that big love out there somewhere. I just haven't found it yet."

I nodded and stood up. "Let's put it behind us. Want to dance?" I asked, holding out my hand in a gesture of friendship.

She let out a laugh and shook her head no. "No way. Go out there and dance with her. I'm waiting for a happily-ever-after here."

I smiled gratefully. Out of the corner of my eye, I saw Dean walk Bethy over to their table. "You won't get the ending tonight. We have so much to overcome," I said, wishing it was that easy.

"I imagine so. But at least, if I'm going to be left with a cliffhanger, make it a good one," Charity said with a teasing grin.

I wanted nothing more than for tonight to end as amazingly as it had started. "Wish me luck," I said, shooting her one last smile before heading across the room to get Bethy.

"Her name is Bethy, right?" Charity asked.

I looked back at her. "Yeah."

"Then I am totally Team Trethy."

What the hell was she talking about? I didn't ask, because I didn't want to waste any more time.

Bethy

Dean was a good distraction. Thad had said Della needed Tripp to entertain Charity. Braden wasn't feeling well, and Charity didn't know anyone else. I understood that and should have been completely fine with it. I should have been relieved, actually. I'd been all over Tripp when Thad snapped me out of it. At some point, the feel of him and his breath against my neck had altered my common sense.

I didn't return to the table with Dean, though. I kept walking. I needed to find a quiet spot and gather my thoughts. Seeing Tripp in close conversation with Charity, their heads bowed together, was too much. I'd been ready to climb into his arms, but he had walked away easily enough.

Ugh. I was being catty. I hated that. I was not that girl.

Once I was out from under the tent, I went toward the darkness and away from the lights and the servers' area. I couldn't go back to my room yet. That would be rude. I just needed a few moments to myself. Maybe a good pep talk before I went back in there.

The cluster of palm trees was the closest thing to privacy I could find, so I headed down the small hill toward them. The sound of footsteps behind me stopped me, and I turned around to see Tripp closing in quickly. What was he doing?

He caught up to me and grabbed my hand. "Keep going," he said as he kept his eyes on the palm trees.

"Why?" I asked, confused, as I started jogging to keep up with him.

He didn't respond. When we were in the shelter of the trees, he grabbed my waist and pushed me up against one of the fat trunks. "Where were you going?" he asked, searching my face like it had all the answers in the world.

His hands were still on my waist, and his grip, although it wasn't painful, was firm. "Uh, well, here," I stammered out.

"Why?" he asked, stepping closer to me.

"I needed a moment alone," I admitted. *And you were all chummy with Charity.* But I didn't say that part. It would confuse things. Tonight was just a moment in time when we could forget the past. Nothing more.

"I was coming to get you to dance again," he said, lowering his voice as he moved in closer and tilted his head down toward me.

"You looked very busy to me," I replied before I could stop myself.

He moved one of his hard thighs between my legs. "I was talking. Did that bother you?"

Yes. "No, of course not."

"Mmm-hmm," he replied as he reached up and ran his thumb over my jaw then behind my ear before letting his fingers trail down my neck.

"Tripp," I managed to say, although my voice was off.

"Yeah, sweetheart?" he replied, now running a finger back up my neck.

"Wh-wh-what are you doing?" I was really stammering now. Oh, God, I couldn't handle this.

He bent his head and inhaled deeply against my neck. "I wanted to do this while we were dancing. Your skin's so soft and smells so damn good."

I wanted to tell him we should stop. This couldn't go anywhere. It would only add to the pain. But my head tilted back, and I arched my neck instead. An open invitation.

Tripp groaned just before his lips touched my skin. The hot tip of his tongue darted out and licked its way up the side of my neck, and then he pulled my earlobe with his teeth gently before kissing his way to my mouth. I knew it was coming, and all I could do was hold my breath in anticipation.

When his lips covered mine, reality ceased to matter. That moment was all that mattered. Tripp's hand reached down, grabbed one of my legs, and pulled it up. I wrapped it around his waist as he moved his leg in tighter between my thighs.

His mouth opened over mine, and I gave him what he was asking for. The taste of tonight's champagne assaulted me as his tongue slid over mine slowly, as if he was trying to savor me. I slipped my fingers back into his hair. I needed to hold him here. I didn't want this to end. This feeling . . . I'd forgotten it. So many times, I thought it was just a young girl's imagination that had made me think it was this good. But my memory needed no embellishment.

Everything else in life fell away when Tripp's mouth was on mine. Tasting him was only part of it. The intimacy of each lick and caress was like a flame being ignited.

Tripp's hands eased up my thighs and under my dress until he was cupping my bottom. He froze, and everything stopped when his hands met bare skin instead of panties. I'd forgotten that I had forgone panties to avoid a panty line.

He inhaled sharply, tore his mouth from mine, and looked down at me. The desire that pounded in my veins and awakened every inch of my body was there in his eyes. "No panties," he said in a hoarse whisper.

I shook my head because speaking was too much.

He slowly slid his hand down until he met the wetness that he'd caused. He lowered his forehead against mine and closed his eyes tightly while his finger began to move between my open legs. His breathing was hard and labored, as if he kept forgetting to breathe and had to gasp when he remembered to.

I squeezed his shoulders and trembled as his finger remained so close to where I wanted it to touch.

"You're soaked," he said, then hissed in a breath.

I was aware of this. I could feel it dampening my thighs. He began to move his finger, and I buried my face in his chest and cried out. He slipped one finger inside, then slowly started pumping it in and out. I moaned and panted, with my mouth muzzled against his chest.

"So hot and tight. God, I love touching you like this. I'm going to rub that swollen clit now, sweetheart. Hold on to me," he said just before his thumb did as he promised.

My head fell back as I screamed out his name.

"Fuuuuck," he said, grabbing my head and pulling it back against his chest. "That good? That hot little pussy wants to be taken care of? You're squeezing my fingers so damn tight I swear I'm gonna end up coming in my damn pants."

I didn't need the added stimulation of Tripp's dirty talk. I was already ready to explode. I wanted to scream his name and claw at his bare back. I no longer cared if someone heard me. I just wanted the release he was going to give me.

I gripped handfuls of his shirt and tried to unbutton it frantically. I needed my hands on him. I wanted to feel that beautiful chest I'd fantasized about.

"Easy," he said, reaching up to keep me from ripping his shirt open. "I'll take it off if that's what you want, but right now, I want to feel you come on my fingers," he whispered, pressing a kiss to my lips.

I wanted that, too.

"You've soaked my leg," he said with a pleased chuckle.

Oh, God. I didn't even care. Grabbing his shirt tighter in my fists, I panted wildly against his chest.

"Ride my hand. Show me what feels good. Fuck my fingers, sweetheart. I've got you." His voice was deep and raspy in my ears.

I didn't need to ride his hand and show him anything. The sound of his voice talking about me fucking his fingers as he did wonderful things to me was enough to send me flying over the edge. The pleasure that broke inside was almost painful as it rocked my body hard. I jerked wildly as Tripp's name fell from my lips in a desperate plea.

His mouth was still at my ear, telling me things that only prolonged this. How he could smell me and how my come was coating his fingers and how hard he was. I had forgotten about his dirty talk. He had a very powerful way with words.

"Stop!" I gasped out, needing to breathe.

He was holding me tightly against him as his hand remained cupped between my legs. "Stop what, sweetheart?" he asked, running his mouth up and down my neck as his heavy breathing heated my skin.

"Don't talk," I begged. He had to stop talking. It was too much.

A low chuckle vibrated through his chest, and I realized I still had his very expensive shirt clasped tightly in my fists. I let go and tried to smooth it out, even though my body didn't want to function properly. "Can I talk yet?" he asked.

I looked up at him as he watched me, the need still glowing in his eyes. "If it's not dirty," I said, still sounding like I had run a mile.

He laughed out loud this time and pulled me tighter to him as his hand slowly eased out from between my legs.

"S'not funny," I said, laying my head back against the trunk of the palm tree.

He bent down and kissed the corner of my mouth. "You don't like it when I tell you how good you feel?"

Oh, I liked it all right. "Your dirty mouth should come with a warning. It's lethal," I informed him as my heart slowed and my breathing evened out.

He smirked, then dropped his eyes to my legs, which were still straddling his thigh. I lowered my leg that I had wrapped around his waist. "My very wet pants leg believes you enjoyed my dirty words just fine," he said, looking back up at me.

I was on my tiptoes in my heels to keep from completely sinking down onto his thigh. My calves were starting to burn. Damn man was too tall. "I need you to move your leg before I get a cramp in my calf," I told him.

"Why will you get a cramp?" he asked, looking down. "Stop standing on your tiptoes. I've got you," he said when he saw what I was doing.

I sighed and enjoyed the oxygen as it filled my lungs. "You're already complaining about your wet leg. It will get much worse. I'm a bit of a mess," I admitted.

"Not complaining about that, sweetheart. It's sexy as hell. I can smell you on me, and it's fucking amazing."

Oh, God, there he went again. I shook my head at him and put a finger over his lips. "No more of that. I mean it. I have to pull myself together and walk back inside."

Tripp grinned, and his lips felt so full underneath my finger that I wanted to trace them and lick them. "You can't go back in there, sweetheart. Your dress is wrinkled, I've pulled most of your hair down, your lips are swollen, and I'd bet the soft skin on your neck is all red from my obsession with it. Then there's the fact that you aren't wearing panties, and you smell like sex. It's intoxicating, and I refuse to let someone else smell it."

Oh. Yeah. I couldn't go back in there. I needed alone time for real now.

"I'm going to straighten myself up and go inside and give our good nights to Della and Woods. I'll make an excuse for you." He stopped and studied me a moment. The look in his eyes made me tingle between my legs again, though that should have been impossible. "Then I'm coming to you. I need you naked, and I want inside you."

He didn't give me time to reply. He dropped his knee and steadied me, then straightened my dress before walking back to the tent. I watched his long legs and the way his wide shoulders looked in that jacket. I waited for the guilt to hit me. I hadn't been with anyone since Jace.

But it didn't come.

Which made me angry. At myself for betraying Jace. At Tripp for making me want him. At life because I knew what I'd had with Tripp was destroyed. It could never be again.

Tripp

Once I was within the glow of the tent lights, I glanced down to check myself. Other than my shirt being wrinkled, I was fine. Besides, I didn't intend to stand around long. I wasn't giving Bethy enough time to change her mind.

Luckily, Woods and Della weren't dancing. They were talking with Rush and Blaire. I slipped around the side so I didn't have to walk through the tables and speak to anyone. Rush's gaze found me first. My wrinkled shirt didn't go unnoticed, and his eyebrows shot up in surprise.

"Where you been?" he asked in a slow, amused drawl when I finally reached them.

The other three pairs of eyes swung to look at me. Woods didn't look thrilled, but Della seemed to be OK about my leaving Charity. A smile tugged on her lips.

"Your, uh, um," Blaire stammered, looking at my wrinkled shirt. She glanced at Rush for help.

He chuckled at her reaction, and Blaire's eyes went wide with understanding.

"Did you and, uh, Charity hit it off, then?" Blaire asked, her voice sounding unsure.

Charity? Fuck no.

"He abandoned Charity a while ago," Woods said in an annoyed tone.

Della looked up at him and slapped his chest. "He did not. He talked to her, and she told him to go. It's OK now, you don't have to be upset with him."

Woods looked relieved. "Good. Let's not set him up on a date again. Too much damn stress."

Della laughed and turned her gaze back to me. "Sorry about all that. I was trying to be helpful. I didn't know . . ." She trailed off.

"It's OK. I know, and I appreciate the thought. Uh, listen, tonight's been great, and I'm really happy for y'all. But Bethy had to go back to her hut, and I'm going to make sure she gets there safely."

Rush tried to smother his laugh with a cough. Woods didn't even try. Assholes. They could at least pretend to believe me for the women's sake.

"Oh, of course. Tell Bethy thank you for everything, and if we don't see y'all in the morning before we take off, we'll see you when we get back from our honeymoon," Della said.

"Have fun," I told her, then glanced over at Blaire, whose curiosity was all over her face. If I didn't get out of there fast, she was going to start asking questions.

"You, too," Woods replied with a smirk.

Before they could see the grin on my face, I turned and headed for the exit.

⌗

Bethy was sitting in the lounger outside her hut as I walked up. She was lost in her thoughts. It didn't look like she had even gone inside. The heels she'd been wearing were dangling from her fingers, but other than that, she hadn't changed. Fear of where her thoughts might be swept over me.

I sat down beside her, but she didn't look at me. Not a good sign. I wanted to reach over and take her hand, but I was afraid she would bolt. I was helpless again. I knew this feeling well.

"He looked like you," she said softly as she watched the water sparkle under the moonlight. "The first day he noticed and flirted with me, all I saw was you. The way he smiled, how his eyes danced with amusement. He was so much like you." She stopped and looked at me. A sadness in her eyes I couldn't reach tore me apart. "I slept with him the first time because of you. I missed you so much."

She needed to do this, but I wasn't sure I could sit through it.

"But he wasn't like you. Not really. He was his own self. His smile was more crooked, and he was playful. Less serious. He loved me, and because of that, I fell in love with him. I was scared at first, to love again. I knew how bad it hurt in the end."

My hands fisted as I forced myself to breathe.

"His love was easy, and he made me feel like the most important thing in his life. I'd never had that before."

Because I'd left her. I hadn't stayed.

"Losing him, losing what we had, was . . ." She dropped her head into her hands and took a deep breath. "It changed me. It almost destroyed me. I don't know if I'll ever find that girl I once was again. The girl I became with Jace." Finally, she turned her head to look at me. "You and I had history. A past that needed closure. I was so afraid when you came back that I loved you more. That I would always love you more. You terrified me. I was so afraid I'd lose what I had with Jace because when I looked at you, my heart did things I hadn't felt in a long time."

She reached up and wiped away a tear that had escaped and rolled down her cheek. If I could go back and change the past, I would. Anything to take this away from her.

"I'll have to live with the fact that my stupidity took his life. That guilt will never go away. I was drinking to numb the memories. I knew I needed to tell Jace the truth about us and the pregnancy, but I couldn't. I didn't want him to hate me. I was afraid I'd lose his love. The way he looked at me like I was the only one in the world for him. But if I could go back, I'd tell him. Even if he hated me for what I'd done, at least he'd still be alive. His laughter wouldn't be gone . . ."

I reached over and covered her hands, which she was fisting together in her lap. Her body tensed under my touch, but she didn't move away. I didn't know what the right words were. All I knew was that Jace wouldn't have wanted this. He didn't die saving her so she could live with this guilt. "You were scared of losing the man you loved because of something from your past. Drinking too much to mask emotions you didn't want to face is normal. People do it all the time. What happened with Jace was not your fault. It was an accident, Bethy. It was a tragic accident. You had been in that water after partying and drinking many times in your life. We all have. Hell, I went surfing at night drunk once. Is that safe? No. But you weren't thinking clearly. Jace saw you go out there, and his only thought was to keep you safe. He never once thought about the danger of swimming out too deep or rip currents. He chose to save you and sacrifice himself. And I knew him well enough to know he didn't want to save you so that you could live with this guilt and pain. He wanted you to have a life, Bethy. He wanted you to live. What you've been doing is not living."

Bethy's mouth puckered up as she sucked in a sob. I would take this all from her and live with it if I could. "Tonight," she said as another sob broke free. "Tonight with you . . . I didn't even think about him." As if realizing it herself as she admitted it, she pulled her hands free of mine and stood up abruptly, putting distance between us.

"That's part of living. Enjoying life. You've just been existing," I told her, hoping she got this. Accepted it.

She sniffed and wiped at her face. "I just . . . I can't." She stopped and took a deep breath, then turned to look at me. "I can't live life . . . with you. I just can't."

I stood up, but she shook her head and turned to go inside. "I love you." The words came out before I could stop them. Those were words I had wanted to say to her again for the past eight years.

She grabbed the side of the door tightly but didn't look back at me. We stood there in silence for several moments while I held on to the one small thread of hope that this would keep her in my life. "I'm sorry, but it's too late."

She walked inside, and the walls around her hut closed.

This was it. I needed to walk away and let her find the life she wanted. I would never be a part of that life. But how could I accept that? I wanted a future with Bethy. I wanted to be the one to make her smile. How much more could I push her? Finding a way to let her move on and heal without me felt like ripping my heart out and leaving it lying there at her feet. She wanted to heal. She just didn't want to do it with me.

Bethy

I set down my tray of drinks and took several deep breaths. It had been three months since I'd successfully pushed Tripp out of my life. When we had returned from the island after the wedding, Tripp no longer followed me to work and back. Unless he was with the guys playing golf, I rarely got a glimpse of him.

"You good, *chica*?" Jimmy, the head server at the club's dining room, asked as he strolled through the double doors.

I managed a nod and plastered on a smile. "Yeah, great," I replied.

"Good, because the board members are all here. We got our hands full tonight, and good ol' Aunt Darla's out there to make sure we don't mess up."

I had already seen the reserved table and the guests sitting at it. That was the main reason I needed a moment to get myself together. Waiting on my friends was normally something I enjoyed doing, because both Della and Blaire had worked here once, too. They were easy to wait on. Most of the time, they got up and fixed their own drinks and got their own plates from the kitchen.

But this was different. They were all dressed up. This was

a business dinner, which Woods held every quarter. Once I had gone to those gatherings with Jace, although being on the outside wasn't really that hard for me.

Seeing Tripp with a date was what threw me for a loop. Not that I even had a right to care.

"Waters are on the table. Woods has already chosen a red and a white for dinner. You take the red, and I'll take the white. I also expect Dean Finlay will order bourbon. Everyone else normally sticks with the wine."

I nodded my head again, still trying to figure out why I was so upset over Tripp bringing a date. I had pushed him away, and it had worked. Maybe too well. He was with London Winchester tonight. They had dated in high school for two years. When we were together, he didn't seem to like her at all. She annoyed him.

But she didn't look like a runway model back then, either. She had to be close to six feet tall, and most of that was legs. Ugh.

"Girl, you sure you're OK? You look pale." Jimmy stopped in front of me and put his finger under my chin to tilt it up so he could see me. There were a lot of beautiful men in this town, but Jimmy quite possibly had them all beat. He was startlingly attractive. The cougars tipped him well and tried their hardest to get him into bed.

Jimmy, however, had a boyfriend. A very hot boyfriend named Ben. It was kept on the down-low, because if the cougars knew Jimmy had no interest in the female gender, then his tips wouldn't be as good. He was an excellent flirt.

"Long day, and waiting on a table where my aunt Darla is sitting doesn't sound like a good way to end it."

Jimmy rolled his eyes. "That woman loves you. Don't be so mean."

Aunt Darla did love me, but she was also hard to please. She ran a tight ship around here. It was one reason she was on the board of directors for the club. Woods knew he needed her. "I know," I replied, and took the bottle of red wine from Jimmy's outstretched hand.

"Get out there." He nudged me, and I put on a smile and headed to the private area of the dining room where the board of directors sat.

A table full of my friends and my aunt shouldn't be so hard to deal with. I should be happy to end my night like this. The tip Woods would leave would pay my rent this month and then some. I should be thankful.

London turned her catlike eyes my way and looked right through me. She wouldn't know who I was, and for that I was thankful. I hadn't kept up with London since that summer with Tripp, so I had no idea what she was doing now. She very likely could be modeling.

"Bethy!" Blaire's excited voice called out. I shifted my gaze from London to her. She was beaming at me as if I hadn't just spent the day with her two days ago. After the wedding, I had done my best to live my life in a way I hadn't in years. Tripp had been right about that. Jace didn't sacrifice his life so that I wouldn't live mine. I had to live for both of us. I was doing my best.

"I heard I missed a shopping trip," Della said, smiling up at me. "I demand a do-over next week."

"If you hadn't been off on a secret rendezvous with your hubby, you could have come, too," Blaire teased.

Della grinned and shot a loving look at Woods.

I glanced around, purposely avoiding Tripp, and realized Harlow wasn't there.

"Where's Harlow?" I asked Grant, who looked lost without his wife and kid.

"Lila Kate isn't sleeping through the night just yet. Harlow naps whenever the baby does, which includes now." Grant gave a yawn of his own.

Rush chuckled. "Been there."

Jimmy nudged my side as he walked up beside me. "Wine," he whispered.

I remembered I wasn't out here to visit and moved to fill Woods's glass with red wine. He never drank white.

Jimmy started at the other end, where Rush was seated.

"I just want some sparkling water," Della said as I moved to her.

I moved on down the table and filled Grant's glass, then my aunt Darla's. Blaire already had white wine in her glass, so I moved on. As I poured, Tripp's voice was the only thing I heard. He was laughing with Woods about something that happened that day on the course. He was happy. Did London make him happy?

London already had a glass of white wine, but Tripp's glass was still empty. I was going to have to ask him if he wanted red. Crap. Why was this so difficult? I was being ridiculous.

"Red wine?" I asked in a quiet voice so as not to draw attention or interrupt anyone.

Tripp turned his head to look directly at me. My heart picked up its pace like it always did when he was near me. Making eye contact with him seemed like a bad idea, but I didn't have much of a choice.

It was a brief moment, but in his eyes, I saw a flash of regret before he nodded his head. "Please," he replied, then looked away to continue his conversation with Woods.

London leaned closer to him, and he put his arm behind her chair. The intimacy between them was obvious. They were comfortable together. They fit. She was tall and gorgeous. Perfect for Tripp. My stomach twisted in knots.

I quickly hurried from the room back to the kitchen, where Jimmy was waiting with a tray of soups. "Cauliflower soup with chanterelle mushrooms and truffle oil. As soon as these are served, we'll need to get out the cheese plates. I'll carry them. They weigh a shit ton. You just follow me and take them off the tray and place them on the table."

"Got it," I replied.

Jimmy winked and headed for the door to hold it open while I carried my tray out. He was right behind me with an identical one.

Once again, I went to Woods, and Jimmy started with Rush. I moved left so Jimmy would have to go right. One fewer thing I had to serve Tripp and his date. Maybe I could work it that way all night.

"What is this?" Della whispered as I placed the soup in front of her.

"Cauliflower soup with fancy mushrooms and truffle oil," I replied.

She scrunched her nose, and I had to bite back a smile.

"It's good. I tried it last week. If you don't like it, I'll have them prepare you something else," Woods promised, and he smiled at her as if she was the most wonderful thing he'd ever seen.

I had to agree with her. I didn't think anything with cauliflower could be good. Not even truffle oil could fix that. Della took a small taste, and I waited to see if I needed to take it back.

"OK, yes, that's delicious," she said, and I moved on to finish placing soups in front of everyone on my side.

This would have been easy if I didn't feel the heat of Tripp's gaze on me the entire time. It was making me nervous. My heart wouldn't slow down, and that stupid knot just got tighter.

Jimmy was waiting for me once again when I got to the door. I opened it and held it so he could walk out with the cheese plates. Once we got to the table, I tried not to make eye contact with anyone while I took the four plates and placed them down the middle of the table. Because Jimmy had stopped on Tripp's side, I had to lean over beside him to put down the tray that belonged to that part of the table.

His arm brushed my side, and I had to hold my breath to keep from making a noise. Flashes of our night against the palm tree came back to me, and my face heated. This was not the time to remember that. I used those memories at night to keep me company in my lonely bed. In the beginning, I'd felt guilty about getting myself off to Tripp's dirty words, but I needed it. And now I accepted it.

Tonight he'd be using his dirty words on someone else.

Tripp

London crossed her legs beside me and rubbed her foot against my calf. Last week, I had been walking from the course to my Harley after playing a round with Woods, and London had been stepping out of her Mercedes, which had been parked right next to me. I didn't notice her at first, but when she'd said my name, I recognized the voice. It was older now, more mature, but it was London.

We had talked, and it had been surprisingly nice. She seemed different now. The spoiled brat I had grown tired of was gone. She had matured and turned into a more confident woman.

And I needed a distraction.

Moving on and letting Bethy go wasn't easy. I thought about her all the damn time.

London was in Rosemary Beach at her parents' place for the next month, so I figured why the hell not—I asked her out to dinner. Since then, we'd been out three times. Tonight made our fourth. She was still wrapped up in a world I wanted nothing to do with, but she liked me. She seemed to enjoy being near me. I had spent so much time being pushed away by Bethy that it was refreshing.

I hadn't realized Bethy was going to be serving our meal tonight. If I had, I probably would have made some excuse to miss it. Seeing her wasn't easy. Putting space between us didn't seem to matter. One look at her, and I was right back to being that guy, desperate to get her to forgive me. To love me again.

During the past three months, I had accepted the fact that she may have been my big love but Jace had been hers. It hurt like hell, but it was the truth. Whoever she ended up with would be second-best. I wasn't sure I could live being second-best for Bethy. Not when she'd always be my number one.

"That server keeps staring at you," London said in an annoyed whisper. Immediately, I snapped my gaze up from the shrimp on my plate to see Bethy taking Blaire's empty plate. Her eyes had been fixed on me, but the second I looked up, she quickly looked away.

Well, what the fuck did that mean?

"See? She's been doing that all night. I was trying to ignore it, but it's getting ridiculous," London hissed. "Do Della and Woods not notice? Is she a friend of Blaire's? They seem real chummy."

I watched as Bethy took the last empty plate and hurried off. Had London not pointed it out, I wouldn't have noticed, because I was trying not to look at Bethy. I had done a damn fine job of it all night. OK, no, I hadn't. Every time she came to the table, I hadn't been able to look away. I was *trying* not to look, though.

"Do you know her?" London asked, getting frustrated. I wasn't answering her questions.

"Yes. She was Jace's girlfriend. She's very close to Blaire and Della," I replied, reaching for my glass of wine.

"Jace dated a girl who works *here*?" she asked, obviously horrified.

I set my glass down and tried not to get annoyed by her tone. She was an elitist. It was how she had been raised. "Blaire and Della once worked here, too. Rush and Woods married them. I don't see how that's an issue."

She gasped. "Ohmygod! You're kidding me! I'm so behind on gossip around here."

This time, I did roll my eyes.

I caught Blaire's gaze as she looked from me to London, then gave me a tight smile before she looked away. I wondered if she'd heard London. Surely not. If she had, Rush would have, and if Rush had heard her, we would all know it.

Woods stood up, and everyone followed suit. Conversations ended, and the women picked up their purses. Della looked at me. "You'll be at the barbecue we're having on Saturday, right? Woods told you about it, I hope."

Woods had sent me a text inviting me a couple of days ago. I nodded. "Yeah, I'll be there."

Della shifted her gaze to London. "Will you be bringing a date?"

London's hands wrapped around my arm as if she was claiming possession. Which was good. Right? I wanted to be wanted. She sure as hell seemed to want me. "Yeah, uh . . ." I glanced at London. "You want to go?"

She nodded, clearly pleased at the invite.

Della didn't look thrilled, but she covered it up well. "Great. See you then."

I said my good-byes to the others and bent my arm so London could continue to hold on to me, since that was what she seemed to want to do.

I was aware that neither Blaire nor Della cared much for London. Neither spoke to her directly, and their facial expressions said it all. They needed to get over it. Bethy had made it very clear that she would never want me. This was me moving on. Just like Bethy wanted me to.

As we walked toward the valet, I heard Bethy's laugh, and my body came alive. It was a sound I hadn't heard in a while. One I loved. One I couldn't fucking get over.

Glancing back, I saw her talking to Jimmy as she walked toward the back entrance. He was making her laugh. I wanted to make her laugh. Jimmy's eyes lifted and met mine. Bethy turned to see who he was looking at, and her smile fell away. She started to trip, and Jimmy grabbed her arm and said something in her ear.

With his arm around her, they disappeared outside.

"Are you ready for your car to be brought around, Mr. Newark?" the valet asked as I stepped outside. We had come in London's car tonight. She wasn't a fan of motorcycles. But I didn't correct the valet. I simply nodded.

"Do you think I can come inside tonight?" London asked as she stared up at me through her lashes. I didn't need her to spell it out. That look told me all I needed to know. If I wanted it, I could have it.

Problem was, I wasn't feeling it. Not after seeing Bethy. "I'm beat," I replied.

"Really? You're *beat*? That's what your excuse is?" She was angry. But I knew she would be. She had taken it well when I'd dodged the last few advances she'd made, and now it was time for her to start getting more blunt. I got that. But I wasn't ready.

"OK. You want the truth? I'm not over my last relationship. I need some time. If you can't deal with that, then we need to end this now. If you can let me deal, then we're good. But don't push me, London," I said, dropping my arm and putting some space between us.

She didn't respond right away. I knew she hadn't been expecting me to blame this on a past relationship. If she only knew it had been eight years since it ended. "I didn't know. You hadn't mentioned anyone."

I let her think about it and decide what she wanted to do. Either way, I was good with it.

The valet pulled her car up, and I turned to her.

"I can get another car home if you prefer," I said, almost hoping that was what she preferred.

She frowned and shook her head. "No. I'll take you home. I'm willing to give it more time."

I wasn't sure I had the energy for this. Using London to distract me from Bethy was wrong. I didn't need to waste her time. I was a lost cause and completely out of reach for what she wanted.

Bethy

Aunt Darla met me at the clubhouse the next morning. The woman never looked concerned, so the worried frown between her brows didn't bode well.

"'Morning, Aunt Darla," I said.

She didn't even pretend to smile. "Come into my office. We need to talk," she said, then turned and headed that way.

I hadn't been called to her office to talk since before I started dating Jace. She'd threatened to fire me if I kept having sex with club members on the property. The truth was, I'd only been having sex with Jace. I had gotten a reputation because of my drinking and partying, but I didn't sleep with more than one guy at a time. Even if I had been accused of it.

I followed her into her office and closed the door. She was standing with her arms crossed over her chest as she studied me. What in the world did she think I had done? My life was pretty uneventful. There had been no partying, drinking, or sex in a very long time, just socializing with good friends.

"What's going on with you and Tripp Newark?" she asked. "I would have thought you knew better than that. Do you remember what happened the last time you messed around with him? I know you've been hurting and missing Jace. I want you to move on as much as anyone else, but not with Tripp. What he did to you is what guys like him do. Jace was an exception. But Tripp will eventually marry well for money. He ran from you once before, Bethy. And left you pregnant." At the word "pregnant," she stopped her tirade and took a ragged breath.

"Nothing is going on with us. What have you heard?" I asked, still unsure who would have told my aunt Darla something. No one had any idea what happened at the wedding.

"I didn't need someone to tell me anything. I was there last night. I watched you looking at him all night long. Then, when he finally took a moment to notice you existed, I saw something in his eyes, too. Don't go there, Bethann. Did you see the woman he was with? That's the type he'll marry. Next time he knocks you up, you may not miscarry. What happens then? We both know you won't go through with an abortion."

Miscarry? What? "Back up. What do you mean, I may not miscarry next time? I didn't miscarry the last time. *You* took me to the abortion clinic. Remember?"

Aunt Darla stiffened, and something flashed across her face that I didn't understand. "Bethann, I never took you to an abortion clinic. I told you that I would help you do something with that baby. You cried for twenty-four hours straight. I made an appointment out of town at an OB-GYN's private office. I didn't want to run the risk of running into anyone who knew us. When we got there, you were cramping. The nurse took you back. The doctor examined you, and the bleeding started. You were only eight weeks along, and you were miscarrying the baby. The doctor gave you strong pain medication that knocked you out and sent you home. When I told you I would help you do something with the baby, I meant the actual baby. I was going to help you find a good home for it. I wasn't going to let you end the pregnancy. That would have haunted you for life . . ." She stopped talking and looked at me with horror in her eyes. "Oh, Bethann. Oh, God, honey. You thought you got an abortion all this time?"

I didn't know there were tears running down my face until she reached over to wipe them away and pulled me into her arms.

"I had no idea that's what you thought. You were so young and scared. I should have explained things to you better."

I held on to her arms as I finally broke down and grieved for the baby I never got to hold. The guilt and shame I'd felt for so long slowly released me, and I cried harder. So many times, I had wished I'd never let them give me the shot that I thought was meant to put me to sleep for the abortion procedure. I had been lying there on that table, thinking about ways I could have the baby. Ways I could make it work. I would beg Aunt Darla. I was going to tell the nurse that I didn't want to do it as soon as she got back. But I couldn't keep my eyes open.

When I'd finally woken up, I was at Aunt Darla's with a thick pad on, and she'd let me know the baby was gone. There was a hollow place inside me from that moment on.

"I didn't kill my baby," I finally said, needing to hear it out loud.

Aunt Darla held me tighter. "Of course not. That's not something you could have handled. I'm not sure I could have lived with myself, either. I just wish I'd known that was what you thought happened."

A weight was lifted. A weight I'd been carrying for eight long years. That one decision I'd thought I made had led to a series of events that destroyed not only me but others around me. The guilt of Jace would never leave me, but I reminded myself daily that he loved me. Even though I was acting insane, he still loved me. He chose for me to live, and I owed that to him. I couldn't let his death be for nothing.

"I want you to go home and rest today. Let this sink in, and spend some time alone. I don't think you're ready to face people just yet. But this doesn't change what I said about Tripp. He left you once, and I watched you crumble. Don't trust him with your heart again."

I nodded. She didn't have to warn me about that. Tripp was moving on. But I had to bite my tongue to keep from defending him. He had been a kid then, too. We'd both been reckless. If he hadn't left, his parents would have shipped him off to Yale. I would have miscarried the baby regardless. It wasn't meant to be. Nothing could have stopped that.

I had nothing to blame Tripp for. The wall I'd built to keep out all the memories that came with him finally crumbled and left me completely raw.

Tripp

Woods had texted me last night to meet him at the course at eight this morning to play a round. I hadn't played golf in years until I moved back to Rosemary Beach. Other than surfing, there wasn't much else to do here. I sucked at it, especially compared to Woods. He played daily.

The truth was, I needed to talk to someone, and this was a good opportunity. When we got together off the course, Della was normally around, and so were other people.

Bethy's face as she looked at me the other night at dinner was stuck in my head, and I couldn't get over it. Either it was wishful thinking, or she looked genuinely upset about London.

Woods was waiting at the clubhouse when I walked up. He didn't have a caddy with him. He never did. He said he didn't need another man to carry his shit and tell him what club to use. I had to agree with him.

He was alone, and although I had expected to see Rush or possibly Grant or Thad with him, I was relieved they weren't there.

"It's just us. Rush was coming, but apparently, Blaire isn't feeling well this morning," he said, tugging the strap of his bag up his arm. "Ready?"

"Lead the way," I said, waving him on.

"Heads-up. Bethy is working this morning. I saw her loading the drink cart when I arrived," Woods said as he stopped at the first hole.

She was here. OK, good. That was good. I could get my water from her. No big deal.

"You and London seeing each other again, huh? Wasn't expecting that," Woods said as he pulled out the driver he needed.

I set my bag down and glanced around to make sure there were no drink carts in the vicinity. This was not a conversation I wanted Bethy to overhear. "We ran into each other here last week. Been out a few times since. I needed to see if I could move on, but I'm not sure I can. It isn't working. I think I'm OK, and then I see Bethy and realize I'm still completely fucked."

Woods nodded, then focused on his ball before taking a swing. It landed and rolled close to the green. Not surprising. "Didn't look like Bethy was real thrilled about you having a date, either. I was worried she was going to dump food on someone, she was so distracted by you."

"That's the thing that fucks me up. At the wedding, we made progress. Real good progress, but she put a stop to it out of the blue. Told me there was no chance, even after I told her I loved her." I lowered my voice for the last part.

Woods's eyebrows shot up. "You told her you loved her?"

"Yeah. I did. I do. I always have."

Woods let out a whistle and shook his head. "Damn, dude. I wasn't going to lie, I had planned on trying to get you to give Bethy one more chance. You seemed so happy the night of my wedding when you came to say good night. Then, watching Bethy ogle you the other night, I figured someone needed to give in. But I didn't know you pulled out the big guns and she shot you down."

That wasn't helping. I jerked a driver out of my bag and walked over to the tee. I didn't have a reply for that. I focused all my energy on beating the hell out of the ball. Unfortunately, that sent it flying over to the nearest trees.

"The hole is that way. Where the flag is," Woods said with a chuckle.

I stalked past him and shoved my club back into the bag. We headed to the trees, since my ball was closer to us. Focusing on this game wasn't going to be possible if I was thinking about the finality of things with Bethy.

"Can I ask you something?" Woods broke into my thoughts.

"Sure, but doesn't mean I'll answer."

"When you think about your future, kids, wife, house, et cetera, who is it you see beside you?"

That was easy. "Bethy. Always has been. Since that summer."

Woods stopped when we neared my ball. Luckily, it wasn't blocked by any trees just yet. It was right there on the edge. I could still salvage this shot. "Things worth having don't come easy," Woods said. "You have to fight for it until you're tired of fighting, and then you take a breather and fight some more." He squeezed my shoulder. "Don't give up. You'll regret it."

❖

I hadn't known how to reply to Woods's advice, but it wouldn't stop replaying in my head. He only beat me by twelve strokes on the front nine, and we were headed into the back nine when the drink cart came over the hill. Woods noticed it, too, and glanced back at me. He didn't say anything, but I could see him silently reminding me of what he had said.

Bethy slowed down and parked the cart. She glanced at me nervously as she stepped down and walked our way.

"'Morning, Bethy. Heard you felt bad yesterday and Darla sent you home. Hope you're better today," Woods said as she approached.

Bethy's eyes shifted to me again, then quickly back to Woods. "I'm better today. Thanks," she replied. "Can I get y'all a drink?" Her focus was on Woods.

"Yeah, I'll take a Gatorade. Blue, if you have it," he replied.

Bethy looked over at me. I wanted to hold her attention, but I didn't want to make her any more nervous than she obviously already was. "Water is fine," I replied.

She nodded and headed back to the cart. I followed her, not glancing back at Woods to see his expression. I wanted to ask what was wrong yesterday, but I didn't want to do that in front of Woods.

She opened the back cooler, then jumped when she saw I had followed her. "Oh," she gasped, and her cheeks turned pink. "I didn't hear you behind me."

I closed the space between us until we were almost touching. "What was wrong yesterday? Are you well enough to be working today?" This was why I'd followed her for so long. No one checked up on her and made sure she was OK. Did anyone fucking take care of her yesterday? Or was she just home sick by herself?

"I'm fine," she said, then paused and chewed on her bottom lip like she wanted to say more. "I, uh, wasn't really sick. I just found out something that sent my emotions into a bit of a spin. I needed some alone time to think."

"What did you find out?" I asked, knowing I was probably stepping over the line she'd drawn.

She glanced over my shoulder at Woods, then looked up at me. "This isn't the place to talk about it."

Well, shit. So she would tell me if we weren't at her place of business? I was half tempted to ask Woods to dismiss her for the day so I could find out what was going on, but she'd be upset. I had pushed her away once already.

"Here." She handed me the water and stepped around me to give Woods his Gatorade.

I watched her walk off. I would be lying if I didn't admit to watching her ass like a starving man. She filled out those shorts really, really well.

"Got nine holes left for me to smoke you," Woods called out when I didn't make a move to return.

Bethy turned around and headed back to the cart. She did good things for the shirt she was wearing, too. Shit. I was getting nowhere with getting over her.

"I have some guys on seven and three I need to serve," she said, climbing up into the cart.

"You're OK today, then?" I needed some kind of reassurance that she wasn't about to jump off a cliff. She had too much already haunting her; she didn't need something new fucking her up.

She smiled, and it was a real smile. Not one of those forced ones I had seen enough of lately. "I'm good. I'm actually better than I've been in a very long time." And then she drove off.

She was better than she'd been in a long time. And I was living in my own personal hell. The one where I got to watch Bethy move on with life without me in it. What would I do when she started dating again? If she got into a serious relationship? This was bad enough.

Bethy

I was as prepared as I could be for this. Della had made sure I knew Tripp was bringing London to the barbecue and that they had been seeing each other. That was fine. I was going to be fine. I could deal with this. Aunt Darla was right—he would have left me again for someone like London eventually. He told me he loved me and within three months was dating someone else. If he'd been sleeping around, having one-night stands, I would have handled it better. But seeing the same girl, the one he was in a relationship with in high school, proved Aunt Darla's point. He wasn't in love with me. If he was, he wouldn't be moving on so fast.

I locked the door to my car and stuck my keys into my purse before heading for the Kerringtons' house. I could smell the barbecue in the breeze. This evening would be fun. My friends were here. And I was a new person.

Della opened the door almost immediately after I rang the bell. She was glowing and more beautiful than normal. When she hugged me, I was a little surprised, but I returned her embrace.

"He's here. Outside with the guys. She's glued to his side. Come into the kitchen with us girls," she whispered in my ear.

I felt bad that my friends thought they had to protect me from Tripp and his date. I had been handled as fragile for too long now. No more. I didn't need their worry or pity. "I'm good. Heck, I'll go have drinks with them outside to prove my point," I said good-naturedly.

Della studied my face a moment and apparently believed me, because she seemed relieved. "Good. Blaire's mixing margaritas. Let's go gossip. Give me your purse, and I'll stick it in the hall closet," she said, holding out her hand.

I gave her my purse and let her put it away while I made my way to the kitchen. Blaire was standing with an apron on over her shorts and blouse, with limes in her hands, which she was squeezing into the blender. Her eyes met mine as I walked into the room, and she grinned. "Good to see your face," she said.

"Ditto," I replied, and took the seat across from her at the bar.

"Harlow just went to get Lila Kate from her stingy daddy. I'm trying to hurry up so I can hold her."

I rarely got to hold Lila Kate. I smirked at Blaire. "Take your time. I can hold her until you're done."

"OK, I got her!" Harlow announced as she walked into the kitchen. "If you want to hold her, you'd better act fast. I'm not sure how long Grant will stay outside before coming in here to hover."

I jumped up and went to take her from Harlow. "Me first," I said as Harlow handed her to me.

"She's not a fan of lying back. She thinks you're trying to make her go to sleep, so she fusses. She likes to see things."

Even at six months old, she was still tiny. Her eyes were

huge and looked so much like her mother's. But she had her daddy's eyelashes and dimple. "Look at how big you are," I said, sitting down with her in my lap. She reached for my hair and grabbed a handful, but she didn't tug on it. She just wanted to feel it.

Her eyes studied my face, and I realized there was no dark twist in my gut. Nothing heavy weighing on me. As much as I loved Nate and Lila Kate, every time I had held them or even been around them before, I'd felt a heaviness on my heart. I'd never wanted to accept it, but I knew why it was there.

But now I was free of that. I could watch her little expressions without sadness or guilt. She let go of my hair and patted my neck. Grant's laughter carried through the windows, and she started straining to see over my shoulder.

"You hear your—"

"Don't say the D word. She'll realize he's not around and start fussing," Harlow warned from her spot at the bar.

That was too cute.

"Enjoy it. I'm almost done, and then she's mine. I have a rambunctious toddler who would rather fist-bump me than hug me, so I need to hold something small and sweet," Blaire said before she turned on the blender.

Lila Kate jumped at the noise and swung her little head around to see what was going on. Her hand squeezed my arm, and she laid her head over my chest. I wanted this. I could admit that now. I wanted a baby. I wanted to be a mom one day. The fact that I could even think about it without having guilt eat me alive was so freeing I almost burst into tears right there in the kitchen.

I ducked my head and blinked away the tears quickly.

Maybe one day, I would explain the past to my friends, but I wasn't ready yet. I hadn't even told Tripp. I had almost expected him to call me and ask me about it after I'd talked to him at the golf course. But he'd either forgotten or gotten too busy.

The blender stopped, and luckily, my eyes dried up. I kissed Lila Kate's face and inhaled her baby smell right before Blaire came over with her hands out and a big goofy grin on her face, saying, "My turn."

I handed her over just as Grant's laughter came through the window again. This time, Lila Kate started trying to twist around to find him. Her lips stuck out, and she scrunched her nose like she was about to cry.

"Oh, no you don't. We don't need him. Come on, let's go explore," Blaire told her as she walked off with Lila Kate in her arms.

Harlow filled two margarita glasses and brought me one. "You want one, Della?" she asked.

Della was washing fruit and putting it into a large bowl. "No, I'm good right now. Thanks," she said.

Harlow bit back a grin and sat down beside me. "You look good," she said.

"Thank you," I replied before taking a sip.

"No, I mean your eyes. You look . . . well, the empty look is gone."

I set my glass down and decided to be as honest as I could without telling them anything. "I'm healing. Learning to let go and live again."

Harlow smiled. "I am so glad to hear you say that."

"Me, too," Della said, then popped a grape into her mouth.

"I'd fix you up, but apparently, I'm bad at that, so I'm not going to try it again."

I knew she was referring to Charity, but that only reminded me that Tripp was outside with London.

"He seems to have found his own date. And he's worse at it than you are," Harlow said with a frown.

"I know, right? I was thinking the same thing," Della replied.

Grant filled the doorway, and his eyes went straight to Harlow. "She OK? Where is she?" he asked, scanning the room like she would be up and walking around on her own.

"Blaire has her. She's fine," Harlow said with a laugh. "Go back outside."

Grant walked over and pressed a kiss to Harlow's head. "You good in here?"

Harlow grinned up at him. "I'm with my friends drinking a margarita. What do you think?" she teased.

"Good point," he said, then pressed a kiss to her lips this time.

"Oh, for God's sake, get a room! You're the worst one of the bunch," Della said, laughing.

Grant flashed a smug smirk.

"Uh-oh, I didn't know you were in here," Blaire said as she walked back in.

Lila Kate got one look at Grant and started reaching and fussing to make sure everyone knew who it was she wanted.

"There's my girl," Grant cooed, and went to take her from Blaire.

"Well, that lasted all of twenty minutes," Blaire drawled as she went over to get a margarita.

"He's getting better," Harlow added.

Lila Kate fisted a handful of Grant's shirt like she was holding on for dear life. Her head was tucked up against his neck. She looked completely content.

"She needed her daddy. Y'all leave us alone," he said in a soft voice as he turned to head back out of the kitchen. "I'm taking her back outside with me," he called out behind him.

Harlow took another drink and shook her head, still grinning as she watched them walk off. "I swear, I'm going to have my hands full when she gets older. He spoils her rotten."

Della walked over and sat down with the bowl of fruit. "I will admit, seeing him with her makes me want to have babies tomorrow."

Everyone laughed, because we knew we were all thinking the same thing. Grant Carter wrapped around a fifteen-pound bundle of pink sweetness would make any female want babies.

Tripp

Grant walked back outside with Lila Kate in his arms. She was tucked up against his chest like it was the only place she wanted to be.

I could have had that.

Dammit, there was that sharp pain that came along with the thought. We had been kids. It wouldn't have been the fairy tale Grant's fatherhood had turned out to be. Shoving that thought aside, I glanced over at London, who was texting. She'd been doing that since we had come out here. Perfecting the art of looking completely bored and messing with her phone.

Della had been generous enough to invite her to stay in the kitchen with them when we arrived, but London had held on tightly to me and declined the offer. So she could come out here to play on her phone, apparently. I reached for the beer Woods had brought me and took a long drink.

"The girls have margaritas inside, London," Grant said. "I'm sure they would be happy to share."

She glanced up from her phone and gave him a flirty smile. She'd done that several times since we'd come out here. "I'm fine out here. Thank you, though."

He shrugged and took his seat, adjusting Lila Kate on his

shoulder. She lifted her head and gave us a brief appraisal before sticking her thumb in her mouth and laying her head back on his chest again.

"Grill will be ready for the steaks in a few minutes," Woods announced, standing up and going over to check on the flame. "Y'all know how your women want their steaks cooked?" he asked.

"Harlow is medium well," Grant said. "I'm medium."

"Blaire and I are both medium," Rush said as he walked behind Nate, who was scrambling up the stairs.

"Medium well," I said, then turned to London. "What about you?"

She glanced up and scrunched her nose. "I don't eat red meat."

I had told the woman we were going to a barbecue. What the hell did she think we were going to eat? "So you're not going to eat?" I asked.

She gave a small shrug. "I'm sure they have salad or something."

Woods cleared his throat and glanced back down at the fire. He was trying not to laugh. "One of you run and ask Bethy how she eats her steak."

"She likes it well done. We've had this conversation with her before. Blaire was appalled and accused her of ruining a good piece of meat," Rush said.

Bethy was here. I hadn't realized she'd arrived.

And the fact that Rush knew how she took her steak annoyed me. I didn't know shit like that. I'd never eaten steak with Bethy.

"I'm going to go see what other sides Della has, and, uh . . ." I stood up, making an excuse to go inside. "I'll be right back."

I didn't wait for London to say she was going with me.

Stepping into the house, I heard their laughter immediately. Bethy's stood out among the others. She was enjoying their company. I almost turned around and went back outside. Seeing me might ruin the happy mood she was in. I never brought a smile to her face. But I wanted to see her.

When I entered the kitchen, Blaire's eyes met mine, and she smiled. "Hey, Tripp."

The other three heads turned in my direction. Although I didn't miss that Bethy's was the last to look my way, I smiled and tried to look casual. "You bored with the male conversation outside?" Della asked.

"Y'all look like you're having more fun in here," I replied.

"Oh, we are," Della assured me.

They all were looking at me as if they wanted to know why I had come into their lair. I had to say something. Staring at Bethy was too obvious. "I was just checking to see what sides you have to go with the steak. London doesn't eat red meat."

As soon as it was out of my mouth, I wanted to pull it back in. Why had I brought up London, dammit? Bethy turned to study her margarita, and Harlow reached for some fruit. Blaire actually glared at me.

I'd pissed off the women. Great.

"Uh, sure. We have strawberry salad, baked potatoes, asparagus, and butter rolls. If I'd known she didn't eat red meat, I could have gotten her some salmon."

Bethy was drinking her margarita like it was water. Her laughter was gone, and it was all my fault. Just because I wanted to see her.

"That's fine. She knew it was a barbecue. She should have

spoken up before now. She can eat the sides. Sure she eats some of that."

"She can eat the spinach leaves out of the strawberry salad. I'm sure that's what she normally eats," Bethy said, and tipped her margarita glass back again.

Harlow's eyes went wide, and Blaire ducked her head to snicker.

No one else said anything.

Was Bethy taking a jab at London? Or was I reading this wrong?

"I'm sure you're right," I finally replied, and Bethy turned her head to look up at me. I was afraid I would see something there that would upset me, but instead, she looked ready to laugh. Her lips pressed together as if she was holding in her amusement. She was making fun of London. My chest tightened. She was jealous. Bethy wasn't exactly moving on after all.

"You should probably get back outside. You left London out there with the men. I'm sure she's bored," Blaire said.

I glanced over at her and nodded. They were kicking me out. I got that.

Right when I opened the door to walk outside, I heard the first laugh. Then the entire kitchen broke into laughter. Smiling, I closed the door behind me.

Woods turned around with an amused look. "What'd you say to make them laugh like that?"

I shrugged. "I'm a funny guy."

"Who lied to you?" Grant asked.

I ignored him and looked at London. "You eat raw spinach?" I asked.

"Yes," she replied.

Bethy

Dinner had been interesting. Thad got there just in time to eat—he'd been caught up in a meeting with his dad. I was relieved to see him. Being the odd one out was awkward, but Thad being there without a date made it OK.

After downing the margarita to deal with Tripp being in the kitchen, worrying about London, I switched to water. I was done numbing myself with the stuff.

Blaire sat across from me, and Della was on the other side of Thad. Tripp and London were at the other end of the table near Grant and Harlow. It made it easier not to look at them.

"I'm glad everyone was able to come tonight. You are our closest friends, and you've become my family," Della said, smiling as she looked over at Woods.

Conversation ceased, and all eyes had moved to Della.

"We wanted to tell you all at the same time, so we figured this would be an excuse to get together and let you all know our good news. I'm pregnant!"

The room erupted in cheers, and Blaire jumped up to throw her arms around Della, while Woods got pats on the back from the men. I moved in behind Blaire to hug Della and congratulate her.

"I'm so happy for you," I said.

"Thank you," she said with a big grin.

Turning around, my eyes caught Tripp's as he watched me. I wondered if he was thinking about our baby. I wanted him to know the truth. Not that it changed anything for him. I had been the one most affected by it. But still, he should know.

I looked away and walked back to my seat. Thad reached over and took my water glass. "Don't drink the damn water. It's contagious. They're all popping out kids left and right."

I laughed so hard I laid my head on his shoulder. He was right. I was beginning to think it was in the water. When I could catch my breath, he patted my leg and grinned. "We have to watch out for each other. The domino effect, you know."

What he didn't realize was that I wanted that life. The one with the husband who adored me and loved our children. Glancing over at Grant, I watched him kiss Lila Kate's head as he held her. Then I watched Nate crawl up into Blaire's lap and wrap his little arms around her neck and squeeze hard.

"You look happier," Thad said, still looking at me.

I turned my attention to him. "I am. It's getting better. I'm getting better."

He nodded and wrapped his arm around my shoulders, then tucked his head toward mine. "We all love you. You know that, right? Even Woods. We all want you happy."

Tears stung my eyes, and I let him hold me a minute. "I'm very lucky," I replied.

"Yeah, you are. We're pretty damn awesome," he teased.

My happy laughter dried up the tears.

⌘

When I pulled into the parking lot of my apartment, the Harley parked under the streetlight and the rider leaning against it caught my attention. It was Tripp. I couldn't see his face, but his height and the bike gave him away.

What I didn't know was why he was here and how the heck he'd beaten me home from the barbecue.

After locking up my car, I walked toward him. He moved away from his bike and headed my way.

"What are you doing?" I asked once he was close enough.

"Wanted to talk to you without an audience. Can I come in?"

Tripp in my apartment. Was I ready for that? Right now, I had no fond memories in my apartment. No one had visited; it was just a place where I slept and hid from the world. Bringing Tripp into it would change that. He would be a part of it.

"Please," he said, his voice pleading.

I gave in. "Sure, OK."

He fell into step behind me as we walked to the stairs.

"How did you beat me here?" I asked.

"I had Thad take me to my bike and let London go on home in her car. She won't ride on my bike, so we never take it."

How did he expect to have a relationship with someone who wouldn't ride on his bike? "Sounds like a winning combination. No red meat or motorcycles. Y'all have a lot in common," I said, trying to keep my voice light.

Tripp stopped walking, and I wondered if I had made him angry. We were almost at my door. I turned to look at him, not afraid of a confrontation. If he wanted to be a baby, then fine. I had only been joking. Sort of. "You don't like London," he said, watching me.

I could lie. But I wouldn't. "I didn't like her eight years ago, either."

He tilted his head to the side and studied me. "I know why you didn't like her then. Why don't you like her now?"

Was he seriously going to do this here? I shrugged and tried to blow it off. Pulling out my keys, I unlocked my door. "She hasn't changed."

My door swung open, and he walked in close behind me, as if trying to crowd me so I couldn't run back outside. I hated that my body tingled when he was close. I needed space, dammit. "You didn't like her eight years ago because she was my ex-girlfriend. You were jealous of any attention she gave me."

I dropped my purse and keys on the table and spun around. "That's true. What do you want, Tripp? You want me to admit that I'm jealous of her now? Because she's with you? Is that what you're getting at? Will that make you feel better?"

His hand shot out and grabbed my wrist, pulling me to him. "Yes, Bethy, it would make my *fucking year*. Because if you're jealous of London, then I still have a chance. And this isn't over."

I had to keep breathing. His hold sent an electric current buzzing through my arm. My heart was in a frenzy, and the butterflies in my stomach were at it again.

"Is that it? Are you jealous of London?" His words came out in a low, husky voice.

I wanted to lie to him, because admitting the truth would open this back up again. I'd closed the door, and he had walked away. But I hadn't been happy. I had missed him. I had stood at my window at night and stared across the street. I'd missed seeing his bike parked there as he watched over me.

Every time I went to my car to leave and he wasn't around, I knew I'd done this. I had pushed him too hard. "Yes," I finally said.

Tripp's jaw clenched, and his eyes flashed with satisfaction. Then the veins on his neck showed up, and I braced myself.

Tripp

Calm. I had to remain calm. But I wanted to haul her into my arms and kiss her until neither one of us could breathe. She was jealous. She cared enough to not like seeing me with someone else. Hell yeah!

"Then what does that mean, Bethy? You wanted me out of your life, and I backed out." I was taking a risk. I knew it, but I had to know.

She looked away from me and focused her eyes on something over my shoulder. "Maybe it means I'll always feel this way." She shrugged. "I don't know. I just know I miss you." She stopped and rubbed her hands over her face and let out a frustrated growl. "I don't know! This thing with us . . ." She dropped her hands and looked at me. "There's something you need to know. Or something I need you to know. I want you to know."

She was breaking down. Her defenses were finally falling away, and if I was going to get a chance to get into her life, this would be it. "I'm listening."

Bethy motioned to the sofa and chair in her small studio apartment. I hadn't even looked around until that moment. This wasn't where she belonged. I didn't want her here. There was paint peeling on the walls, and the blinds were broken. Masking tape lined the window, and her sofa was patched several times. I kept my face neutral. I didn't want her to think I looked down on her because of where she lived. I just hated knowing that while I went to bed at night in a luxury condo, she was here with bolts and chains on her damn door.

Bethy sat down on a vinyl chair that had seen better days back in the seventies. I took a seat on the sofa.

"I didn't have an abortion. I miscarried," she said.

That snapped me out of my unhappy thoughts about her apartment. "What?"

She let out a sigh, and her shoulders relaxed. "My aunt Darla said she'd help me do something with the baby. I thought that was her gentle way of telling me she'd take me to get an abortion. I curled up in a ball and cried for two days after that and grieved for the baby I didn't know. I didn't want an abortion, but I was sixteen, and my father would never allow me to have a child. My aunt Darla was all I had, and if she was taking me to get an abortion, then I had no one in my life who would support my decision to have a child. I called you several times in hopes you could help me, but I never got through to you.

"When I was eight weeks along, my aunt forced me to go to a clinic; I assumed it was an abortion clinic. I'd never been so terrified in my life. All morning, I had been cramping, but I figured it was from all the crying and the knots in my stomach. Then the doctor examined me, and I was bleeding. I didn't know about that until this past week. I was given a shot for the pain because I was in the middle of an early miscarriage. My memories of that moment got muddled by the drugs.

"When I woke up, I was at Aunt Darla's, and I was bleeding heavily. She told me the baby was gone, so I assumed they'd performed the abortion while I was under. We never discussed it, because it was too painful. This past week, Aunt Darla said something about my miscarriage, and I was confused. She told me the real story. She said she never would have made me get an abortion."

She finally stopped talking and dropped her eyes to her hands.

"I've blamed myself and lived with that guilt for so long when I never had to. I wanted you to know the real story. That I hadn't wanted to abort our baby. That when it was time, I was ready to do whatever I had to in order to keep it."

I swallowed a lump in my throat, overwhelmed by Bethy's story. Not once had I blamed her. I had gotten drunk and remained that way for more than a week when I had finally gotten up the nerve to listen to my voice mails. I'd no longer had my phone with me, the one my parents had paid for, but I could access the voice mail remotely. When Bethy's desperate pleas for help had ended with a final message saying she'd had an abortion, my world had stopped.

I'd thrown a chair across the room at the cheap hotel I'd been staying at and shattered it. Then I'd put my hand through the Sheetrock before falling to my knees and sobbing. My next step had been to drink. I'd had to numb the pain. Bethy wouldn't want me to come back and get her, like I planned. I'd destroyed her. I'd destroyed me. I couldn't face her.

But never had I blamed her. She'd been so young and scared. Her father was hardly ever home, and she worked a job to help pay the bills. I hadn't been listening to voice mails,

afraid to hear what my parents had to say. As a result, I'd ruined my life.

I needed to tell her the truth about why I left. Now.

"Bethy, if I had stayed here, my parents would have sent
me to Yale. I would have spent more than four years there. On
holidays, they would have made me go with my family to Bos-
ton. Then the summers would've been spent at the law firm in
Manhattan. My days at Rosemary Beach were over.

"So I had to run. If I ran away and found a way to become
independent from them, then they wouldn't have any power
over me, and I could come back and see you. Then, when you
turned eighteen, you could come with me. That was the only
answer I could find. I didn't want to lose you."

I watched her face as she listened to me. I had tried to explain this to her so many times. But this time, she was listening
to me. Finally.

"As for the pregnancy, I wasn't using the phone my parents
paid for. I left that behind. I was saving money to get my own.
I was going to call you as soon as I had it. But I was worried
about you, and after a month, I used a phone in my hotel room
to listen to my voice mail. That was when I got all your mes-
sages. My world fell apart in that room."

Bethy let out a sad laugh and shook her head. "We were so
young then. Do you even remember those kids? I forgot how
it felt to be them that summer."

I hadn't. "We may have been kids, but what I felt for you
was real. It never changed or faded. Not once."

We sat there, neither of us speaking, as the sound of the
cars on the street and the neighbor's music above us filled the
silence between us.

I watched her, and she stared off at the wall, lost in thought. So much had changed since that summer when she'd walked into my life and lit it up.

"What I said when we were on the island—I was wrong," she said, swinging her gaze back to me. "I was terrified because I had done the things we had done and not once felt guilty about it. I hated myself for not feeling guilty. But I do want to live my life. Walking through it numbly is lonely, and you're right, Jace wanted me to live." She paused and closed her eyes tightly. "I think, that is, if you want to, I think I'd like us to see each other more. Not exclusively, just casual. Maybe. If that would be something you would want to do."

Not exclusive? Fuck. I controlled my reaction and kept my expression neutral. She was offering me an olive branch, or at least a very small twig, but it was something. It was better than what we had right now. "Yeah, I'd like that," I replied.

She smiled, and the relief in her eyes made everything worth it. "Really?" she asked, as if I was going to change my mind.

"Absolutely."

She looked around awkwardly with a silly grin on her face, then glanced back at me, unsure. "Is it OK if I . . . hug you?"

I held my arms open. "Come here," I told her, and she waited a split second before she wrapped her arms around me.

I inhaled and held on. Dipping my head down, I ran my nose up her neck and grinned as she shivered.

I wasn't her number one, but that didn't change the fact that she was mine.

Bethy

If a guy were to order takeout and rent a movie, would you be interested in joining him?

I grinned down at the text message. Since our talk the other night, Tripp had sent me a couple of random texts but nothing else. I hadn't been sure if he was busy or if he was just testing the waters. This text cleared the air a bit.

I put the golf cart into park so I could respond.

Depends on the guy asking. I have standards.

After I pressed Send, I tucked my phone into my shorts pocket and jumped down to unload the leftover stock. My shift was at an end, and the sun was setting, so the course was closed. The last group had just finished up.

When my phone vibrated, I quickly pulled it back out.

He's tall, extremely good-looking, great smile, knows you like the chicken fettuccine alfredo at Gambino's, and intends

to have that and a glass of white wine waiting for you when
you get to his place.

I laughed out loud, then looked around to make sure no
one saw me smiling like a loon at my phone.

Sold, I typed. I'd go anywhere for that fettuccine.

His response was fast.

Score. See you at seven?

I replied: OK.

I tucked my phone back into my pocket and got to work.
I needed a shower and a change of clothes before I went over
there. I smelled like suntan oil and sweat. Not to mention the
beer that had spewed all over me earlier. Occupational hazard
of working as a drink-cart girl.

I managed to get everything unloaded in record time and
get out of there without Aunt Darla asking where I was off to.
She didn't approve of Tripp, and although she was holding
something against him that happened years ago, I wasn't sure
she would let that go. I would deal with her when I had time.

I made it to my apartment, took a shower, and changed
into a pair of leggings and a top that hung off one shoulder. It
was comfortable and cute. I didn't want to dress up to watch
a movie at his house. That seemed like I was trying too hard.

This was supposed to be an easy thing.

By the time I pulled up to his apartment, it was five after

seven. His Harley was parked outside, and all the lights in his apartment were on. The first time I had walked back into that apartment after his return had been hard. Jace had wanted to throw him a welcome-home party, and I had to pretend I hadn't lost my virginity on his sofa. Or slept in his bedroom more nights than I could count.

Now I was walking back in there to spend time with Tripp. Facing those memories was terrifying. But that was our past, and I didn't have to hide from it.

I knocked on the door, and I could hear Tripp's footsteps as he came down the hall. When the door swung open, the sight of him caught me a little off-balance. Sometimes I forgot just how sexy the man was until he was there in my space again. No wonder my sixteen-year-old heart had been stolen by him.

His hair was damp, and I could smell the fresh soap on his skin. A gray T-shirt clung to his chest in a few places where he hadn't completely dried off before pulling it on. The jeans he was wearing hit his hips so perfectly I was sure they had been made just for him, so that women everywhere could lust over the way his flat stomach rippled and cut into a V as it disappeared into the denim. The jeans also did wonderful things to his long legs. The muscles in his thighs flexed easily as he shifted his stance. Then there were his tanned bare feet, which shouldn't have been a turn-on but totally were.

I snapped my gaze back up to meet his after openly ogling him at his front door. I was thankful that he wasn't smirking at my lapse. He grinned and stepped back for me to enter. "Just now pouring the wine," he said as I walked in, his clean scent meeting my nose.

Why did that make me want to lick his neck?

"I waited for you to rent the movie. I wasn't sure what you wanted to see. I've got iTunes pulled up on the television so you can scan through it and rent what you want."

I walked toward the kitchen, which led into the living room. "I'm in the mood for an action film," I said, thinking that I didn't need to watch anything romantic with him. I had been thinking about licking his neck. I didn't need to see anything to inspire me.

"Like I said, your pick," he said as he stepped back into his kitchen.

I stood on the other side of his bar and watched as he fixed us both plates. He'd ordered the same thing as me, which reminded me of the times he took me out to eat that summer. He always said I ordered better than him and ended up eating off my plate and ignoring his own food.

"Wine." He pushed a glass toward me.

"Thanks."

He picked up the plates and nodded toward the French doors leading out to the balcony. "Want to eat out there? It's prettier than in here."

"Yeah. Let me grab your glass, and I'll get the doors," I said, reaching for the glass he had poured for himself.

We walked outside onto his balcony, and although the furniture out here was different now, my mind still went back to the first time I'd been out here with him. He set the plates down, and I shoved the memory away as I sat down in the chair closest to me. Remembering how we were then would only confuse things now.

Once Tripp was in his seat, he looked over at me. "Not gonna lie, ordering takeout from Gambino's brought back some really good memories." He was doing it, too. Our past would always be there.

"I haven't had this in . . . well, it's been a while," I admitted. Because eating it had always reminded me of him. It wasn't until Jace had started taking me there that I was able to enjoy it without the memories hurting too much.

Neither of us said anything as we began to eat.

Bringing up Jace wasn't something I wanted to do. It wasn't fair to Tripp. We had talked about Jace enough. His memory would always be there. This was about us now.

"What was the most exciting thing that happened today?" Tripp asked, and my eyes shot up to meet his. The flicker in his eyes as he held my gaze caught my breath. So many emotions in those green depths.

Every day that summer, when he had picked me up from work, he would look at me and ask that question. It had started as his way of asking me about my day and turned into my weaving ridiculous tales that never really happened just to make him laugh. In the end, I would reach for his hand and tell him that him waiting for me in the parking lot was the most exciting part of my day.

I held up my forkful of fettuccine. "This is by far the most exciting thing that happened today. Unless you count the fact that I rode up on Mr. Wickingham taking a leak on the tenth hole."

Tripp winced, then burst out laughing.

Tripp

A sense of warmth wrapped around me, and I inhaled the scent of vanilla deeper. Needing to hold on to it. My arms tightened, and the silky-smooth softness I held in my arms made a noise that reminded me of a purr.

That woke me up. Squinting against the sun's rays coming in through the windows, I took in the sight of Bethy sound asleep and snuggled up against me. Her legs were tangled with mine, while the rest of her body was half on top of me as I lay on the sofa.

We had watched the movie last night, or at least tried to. Bethy had lain over on me at one point, and I was unable to do anything but watch as her heavy eyelids fluttered closed. While asleep, she had moved closer to me, to the point where I had to lie down so she could stretch out. The rightness of having her in my arms again as she slept gave me a deep sense of contentment.

Preparing myself for the moment she opened her eyes and realized she'd slept on top of me was another thing. She would be angry. At least, I thought she'd be angry. After three glasses of wine on the balcony and laughing at her stories of when Blaire first came to Rosemary Beach, Bethy had relaxed considerably last night.

I just liked hearing her talk, finding out all that I had missed in her life. She told me about moving out of her dad's house when he married a lady name Renee, who hated Bethy on sight. My chest had ached as I listened to her make jokes about sleeping on the floor and eating noodles for months.

I had eaten my own share of noodles and slept on floors, too, but that was something I never wanted for her. When I rode out of town, I had been determined to build a life somewhere safe, with everything she needed.

I didn't want her to wake up and be upset about this. I hadn't slept so well in years, and I sure as hell hadn't woken up this damn happy in what felt like forever. We hadn't even kissed last night. I wasn't pushing her. My eyes had kept fixating on her lips as she talked, but I would mentally shake myself and force my gaze back to her eyes.

One of her legs stretched out, running down over mine as she began to stir. I eased my hold on her when I realized I'd pulled her to me so tightly it was probably what was waking her up. My subconscious was trying to keep her here in this spot. She let out a soft yawn, and the fingers she had sunk into my hair during the night began to move. Then she went completely still, and I knew my Bethy was finally awake. I gave her a moment to assess things. Yes, she was all kinds of tangled up with me, but we were fully clothed, and nothing was touching anything it shouldn't. When she turned her head and buried her face in my chest, I smiled. Maybe she wasn't going to jump up in a panic.

"I'm so sorry," she mumbled against my shirt.

"For what?" I asked, smiling down at the top of her head.

She let out a groan that was beyond adorable. "I fell asleep on you."

I shifted and tilted her head up so I could see her face. "Never apologize for that. Ever."

She studied me a moment, then licked her lips and dropped her gaze. "I'm smothering you. Can you even breathe?" She still sounded embarrassed. She started to get up, but my arms tightened around her. I wasn't ready for that just yet.

"I slept better than I've slept in years. You're the best blanket I've ever had," I teased, trying to ease the nervous stiffness in her body. I had liked her all soft in my arms. I wanted that back.

She let out a laugh and dropped her forehead back to my chest. "Wine after a long day in the sun knocks me out," she said with an apologetic tone still in her voice.

"Then I'll have to remember to do that often. What are you doing after work tonight?"

She lifted her head, and the smile on her lips made my heart clench. That was my Bethy smile. The one she used to give only to me. "Seeing you two nights in a row isn't casual dating," she said, as if I needed reminding. I didn't want to think about what that meant. She didn't want to be exclusive, which meant she could date other people. If that actually happened, I wasn't sure I could be held responsible for my actions. The idea of her out with anyone else drove me crazy. I wasn't letting that happen. How the fuck I was going to stop it was another thing.

"Sure it is. We ate, talked, watched a movie, and fell asleep completely clothed. That's very casual. Let's do it again tonight."

The smile on her face grew, and she shifted again. Reluctantly, I eased my hold so she could stand up. If I held her down, she might not come back. I could always tie her ass to the bed. That would fix this casual-dating shit.

Bethy stood up and raised her hands over her head to stretch, leaving me with a small glimpse of the smooth skin of her stomach. The leggings she was wearing molded to every curve, and I was close to begging her to turn around and stretch again so I could see her ass in them. The shirt she wore almost covered it up. Last night, all I got was a hint of what it was covering up.

"Today is my day off. I have to do grocery shopping, clean my apartment, and—"

"Go visit Nate, stop by the post office, and get your mail. Then you go to the beach and stand in the spot where we lost Jace," I finished for her. I had followed her for months. I knew her typical schedule for her day off. I didn't want to remind her of Jace, but he was a part of her life. Our life. I wanted to remember him. I wanted to be able to say his name without worrying that she would shut me out.

She blinked at me as if she was surprised that I knew all of this, but there was no sadness there. The guilt and regret didn't cloud her eyes. She turned to walk over and pick up her shoes and slip them back on. It wasn't a secret that I followed her. She knew that.

Sitting up, I ran my hand through my hair but decided I didn't care if it was messy. I leaned forward, resting my elbows on my knees, as I watched her search for her purse. She needed to put space between us, and if I wanted this to happen again, I was going to have to let her.

"Tomorrow night?" I asked, knowing she didn't need me to elaborate on what I wanted.

She turned back to me, and I could see the wheels turning in her head.

"There's a birthday party for Mr. Emerson at the club to-morrow night. He's turning eighty. People are coming in from out of town. It's a big thing. Woods asked me to work it."

Mr. Emerson was London's grandfather. Bethy's eyes said what she wasn't saying. She expected me to be there with London.

I'd actually forgotten about London's asking me to go with her. I had turned her down. After the barbecue, I knew I was wasting my time and hers. She didn't fit into my world. We had been good together once, but I had broken away from that life, and being near London reminded me of why I'd run from it.

"I won't be there. There was nothing to end in the first place, but I told London we weren't going to work. She's a part of a world I don't want."

The relief in Bethy's eyes flashed before she covered it up by glancing away. "Oh, OK," she replied.

"After the party?" I asked. I wasn't giving up.

She fiddled with the hem of her shirt. "I'm always so exhausted after a big event at the club, so I won't be much company. I'll just want to eat and sleep."

I was completely OK with that. "I'll feed you and give you a killer foot massage, then let you go to sleep."

The internal battle playing out across her face had me holding my breath. "OK. But you don't have to supply the food. We get sent home with tons of leftovers from these things. I'll have plenty for both of us."

Mentally, I jumped up and punched the air with a shout of victory. In reality, I managed to stand up calmly and nod my head toward the kitchen. "Great. You want some coffee before you leave?"

Bethy

I held my shirt up to my nose one more time before I pulled it off and inhaled. It smelled like Tripp. And he smelled wonderful. Closing my eyes, I let myself remember how good his hard body felt under mine when I had woken up.

I vaguely remembered being unable to hold my eyes open last night and leaning over to lie on his shoulder. I wish I'd been awake for more of that. I felt like I had missed out. But then, if I'd been awake, there was no way I would have slept on him.

Wearing this shirt all day was tempting, but that would make me creepy. I pulled it off and started to throw it into the dirty clothes hamper and stopped. I dropped it onto my bed instead. I was sleeping in it tonight, and I wasn't going to let myself think about how weird that was.

Agreeing to go over to his house again so soon was probably a bad idea. It made things appear as if they were moving too fast. I had to protect my heart with this man. I already knew he had the power to shatter me. But when he had said he wasn't seeing London anymore, I had caved.

Knowing he didn't want to be a part of the world she lived in eased my mind. Tripp never spoke of his parents, and they didn't live in Rosemary Beach. They hadn't been in Rosemary since Jace's funeral. But summer would be back soon. What if they returned? Tripp hadn't had to deal with them yet. Would they push him? Would he run away again? I couldn't get onto his bike and ride away. Even if he asked me to. My life was here. My job, my friends, my security blanket. Everything was here.

Protecting myself wasn't going to be easy. It wouldn't take much for me to lose myself in Tripp again. Just like last night: sleeping in his arms had come as naturally as breathing. It had felt right.

My heart wasn't safe with him. Even if my body had other ideas.

Today I needed space. I would do my usual routine and distance my thoughts from Tripp.

✠

While shopping for groceries, I bought dill-flavored Pringles and peanut-butter-cup ice cream just in case Tripp came over. Those were his favorite snacks, or they had been when he was eighteen. As I cleaned my apartment, I made a note of things I needed to get to make the place look better. Like a blanket to go over the sofa and maybe some new curtains for the windows. I also cleaned things I rarely noticed, like the baseboards and the fronts of the cabinets. I scraped the paint that was peeling and sanded the wall. I hung a wedding photo that Della had sent me of her, Blaire, Harlow, and me over the spot.

Instead of splurging on paper towels, fabric softener, deli turkey meat, and triple-ply toilet paper, I used that money to buy the body wash and lotion I had been coveting at the new shop in town. Then I picked up a bouquet of daisies before I went to the beach.

It wasn't until my feet hit the warm sand that I realized all the choices I had made today revolved around Tripp. I stopped just before I reached the spot where I had stood the night Jace never came out of the water. Looking at the flowers clutched in my grip, I swallowed the lump in my throat.

Daisies had been the one thing about my time with Tripp that I hadn't been able to let go of. They had been the first flowers anyone had ever given me. Tripp had arrived one night on his bike at my trailer to pick me up, and he had pulled a bouquet out of his jacket. They had been a little smashed, but to me, they had been perfect.

Once a week, Tripp had daisies waiting for me somewhere. I had found them in my locker at work, on my front porch, and at a table he'd reserved for us at the club one night. He'd told me daisies reminded him of me. They weren't overdone and expected, like roses. They were beautiful and free. They lightened up a room, and although they appeared innocent, there was a wildness about them.

When Jace had given me roses the night he told me he couldn't lose me and that I was more than just sex for him, that he loved me, I had told him that daisies worked better on me. From then on, he had gotten me daisies, never knowing his cousin had given me daisies first.

I walked the last few steps until I was back at the place where I'd lost my soul. Staring out at the water, I closed my eyes and let the wind and the sound of the waves wrap around me. A grave wasn't where I wanted to imagine Jace. It was cold and dark in a grave. I believed his spirit stayed here near the ocean he loved. This place made him happy. It was where he'd want to be.

"I brought daisies," I said. The beach was empty, and my words drifted off in the wind. "I know it was you who always gave me daisies, but I needed to bring them to you today." I paused and took a deep breath. "Because I need to tell you something. I want you to understand, and I need your forgiveness.

"I never told you why I loved daisies. You always made jokes about me not wanting roses. I should have let you give me roses. But I loved daisies."

The wind blew some petals loose as I stood there, watching the waves crash against the sand. "I loved daisies because, before you, before us, I had a love that was big. One that was so big it held on all these years, even though you came into my life and found a part of my heart I didn't know was left and claimed it. You don't know it, but you saved me . . . twice.

"I don't want you to think I wasn't completely with you when you held me, because I was. The love that had found me before was there, but my heart was yours then. It was us. I didn't know how to tell you about Tripp . . ."

A daisy blew free of my grasp, and I watched it drift away, then tumble along the white sand before a wave pulled it out into the water.

"I hated him for leaving me. I hated him for things I shouldn't have, because he was a kid, too, back then. There were misunderstandings and pain that ran deep. I was lost, and the girl I had been was gone. You found her and kept her from complete destruction, because that was the course I was on. We were perfect but for only a season. Because Tripp came back. And when he did, it tilted my world.

I waited for the tears to come, because they always did. But today there was no burn in my eyes. No pain in my chest.

"It should have been me who drowned that night. Not you. Me. But you didn't let that happen, because, again, you saved me. I didn't deserve to be saved, but you never seemed to see it that way.

"You took a piece of me when you left. That part of my heart that you claimed is still with you, out there. It always will be. You were my hero."

I looked back down at the daisies in my hand and bent down to place them on the sand. I didn't let them go yet, because the moment I did, they would blow away.

"He's been patient with me. He's watched over me when all I did was push him away. I've said hurtful things to him and wanted to hurt him as much as I was hurting, and he still didn't leave. He just waited.

"When I needed to be saved from the darkness that losing you had put me through, he's the one who saved me. He's made me laugh again. He's made me feel again. And I want to live again. If I live my life, that doesn't mean I'll forget you. That won't happen. What we had will never leave me. You will never leave me." I stood up, leaving the daisies on the sand until each of them was caught by the water and pulled away.

"Thank you, Jace Newark. For loving me, for saving me, for being my hero."

One lonely tear caught my eyelash and rolled down my cheek. I didn't wipe it away. It would be the last tear that I left here, and that made it special.

Tripp

Bethy's eyes had closed thirty minutes ago, but I was still sitting there with her feet in my lap as she lay on my sofa, wearing a pair of cutoff sweats and a T-shirt that she'd brought to change into. She had been different tonight. Her smile had been easier, and there was a lightness to her laugh. Letting her close her eyes and go to sleep had been hard. I wanted to hear her voice and soak in the sound of her laughter.

When she'd arrived with a change of clothes, I'd sent her to the bathroom to take a shower. She had sagged in relief. I had fixed our plates from all the leftovers she'd brought home and listened to her tell me about her evening. When she'd told me that London was there with some guy, she had watched me carefully, as if it would upset me. I'd pulled her feet into my lap then and started my promised massage while teasing her about her long shower.

I dropped my gaze to her feet and remembered the first time I had noticed them. They were dainty, with cute little short toes. She had hot-pink nail polish on them tonight. Back then, they had been bare. Never had I wanted to kiss a girl's feet until I saw hers. The first time I had brought her toes to my lips, she'd giggled and squirmed, trying to get away.

I had told her the only thing I loved more than her was her feet, and she had blushed, covering her face with her hands. I never touched anyone else's feet.

Picking up one perfect foot, I pressed a kiss to the arch, then placed it back on my thigh before shifting her so I could slip in behind her and pull her against my chest. She moved as soon as I lay down, and I was afraid I had woken her up. I went still and waited while she rolled over and proceeded to curl up against me, throwing a leg over my thighs and slipping an arm over my waist. Then she nuzzled her head against my neck and murmured something about me smelling good and not changing her shirt.

I held in my laugh and waited until I was sure she was sleeping before settling in and pulling her closer to me. Sleep came easily and peacefully.

⊞

It was Bethy's breathing and the heat of her gaze that woke me this time. I opened my eyes and noticed the sun hadn't completely risen, so the soft morning glow washed over Bethy's face as she stared at me. We were once again completely tangled together, but this time, she didn't try to squirm away. She had always been a snuggler. That was also something I had never allowed after her. I couldn't sleep with a woman touching me. That right had belonged to Bethy.

"Hey," I said, my voice husky from sleep.

The way her chest rose and fell caught my eye, and I saw the pulse in her neck quicken. Was she upset about something? I swung my gaze back to her face.

"You OK?" I asked, afraid she'd move away from me now.

I had wanted another morning of holding her while she slept.

She gave me a small nod, but her breathing was short and fast. Something was definitely wrong. I moved my hand, which was currently pressed against her back, and slid it away, thinking maybe I was holding her too tightly. But when I slipped it closer to her side, she sucked in a breath. I paused and moved my gaze to my hand. It was resting on her side, but it was just below her breast.

Was she . . . I jerked my gaze back to hers, and then I saw it. The need and desire. Her eyelids lowered as she breathed in deeply. I didn't want to read her wrong, but the idea of her being turned on had my blood pumping hard into my already-stiff cock.

"Ah," she said softly, and closed her eyes.

The swell of my erection was barely brushing her, but during the night, she'd thrown a leg over my leg and moved over me again until her heat was directly against my hard-on. I had a feeling it wasn't just morning wood; my body was reacting to her crotch pressing against it in my sleep.

I lifted my hips just enough to press more firmly against her, and her eyes flared as she grabbed my shoulder. "Does that feel good?" I asked, slipping a hand over her ass so I could shift her further on top of me.

She nodded as I settled her so that her spread thighs were now straddling me and opening her up further. "Oh, God," she moaned as the pressure between us made complete contact.

Reaching up, I pushed her hair back and held her face in my hands. "Did you wake up needy?" I asked, my voice now dropping from arousal instead of sleep.

She didn't respond, but she rocked against me, and her head fell back as her mouth went slack. God, that was sexy. Her boobs were bouncing from all the heavy breathing she was doing, and I wanted them bare so I could watch them jiggle. I reached for her shirt, and she lifted her arms as I pulled it off, leaning up to undo her bra and quickly discard it.

They were so fucking gorgeous. They were bigger now, but her nipples were still that rosy color, and the softness was heavier. I had always been a fan of more than a handful. Bethy's were a couple of handfuls.

She made appreciative noises as she continued to work herself over me, drawing pleasure from the friction. I pinched her nipples and licked at each hard pebble as they bounced in front of me, and she stilled, allowing me to pull one into my mouth and suck.

Her hands went to my head, and she said my name on a whisper. I sucked harder before pressing my face between them and licking up the middle, then moving to the other one to give it just as much attention. Best fucking tits in the world.

"I want your shirt off," she said, panting as her hands started pulling at my T-shirt. I pulled back and kept my eyes on her breasts, not wanting to miss any of their movement as I helped her get my shirt off. Then I went right back to licking and sucking.

Her hands ran down my chest, and her nails scraped up my back as I kept her soft, plump globes pressed as close to my face as I could. When her hips started making needy little circles as she whimpered, I grabbed her waist and stood up with her. She clung to me, wrapping her arms and legs around me, as I went straight for the bedroom. We hadn't been in here together yet, but I wasn't taking her on the damn sofa. I had dreamed and fantasized about this for years.

I laid her down, grabbed her shorts and panties, and jerked them off with one hard tug before moving to crawl over her. "Open your legs for me, sweetheart," I demanded as I touched her thighs and shoved them as far open as I could get them.

Bethy didn't stop me. She let them fall open. Sucking in a breath, I took in the obvious wetness coating her pink folds.

I inhaled deeply, and her arousal filled my senses. "Shit, baby, that smells so good," I said as I moved to press a kiss on her bare mound. She made a pleading noise in her throat. Another time, I'd make her ask me to taste her, because that was hot as hell. But right now, I needed this more than she did.

I ran my tongue up through the middle and then rolled it around her swollen clit while she arched off the bed and screamed. Her hand was once again fisted in my hair as if she intended to hold me here and not let move. The idea of her forcing my head between her legs made me throb harder.

I began to taste and nibble, enjoying the sweet taste I'd missed and the smell that was all Bethy. My name fell from her lips in a chant, and I soaked in the sound of it. When she finally cried out and began to shake through her first orgasm, I held her down and licked it up, tasting her release as she pleaded with me to stop.

When the tremors stopped, she was making noises from the pleasure that I knew verged on pain as I licked at her sensitive clit. Just a little more, and she'd shoot off again, but I wanted inside her first. I crawled over her, and the lazy look she gave me as a smile curled her lips took all other rational thought away.

With one move, I sank all the way inside her. Her nails clawed my back as she arched into me and shouted my name. The tight walls of her heat gripped me, and I lowered my mouth and molded it to hers before moving inside her. She pulled my tongue into her mouth and sucked, making my ability to slow down impossible. Having Bethy sucking anything on my body sent me into a wild frenzy.

"Fuck, oh, fuck, that's so good," I said, tearing my mouth from hers so I could gasp for air. "I swear, I'll never get enough of this." I panted as I watched her breasts bouncing with each thrust. "Fuuuuck. Look at you. God, baby," I growled, unable to get enough. I wanted deeper. I wanted to be so buried in her that I marked her body as mine.

"Please, harder," she begged, her eyes glazed over with pleasure.

Yes! Harder, deeper, more. I needed more. I needed all of her. I pulled out, and she cried in protest before I flipped her onto her stomach and jerked her hips up. "On all fours," I demanded.

She was up and pushing back for me to take her immediately. "Back inside me," she moaned.

I grabbed her ass and sank back inside, sliding deeper from this angle. Letting my head fall back, I roared as she began milking my cock with each plunge.

Leaning forward, I grabbed both her tits and squeezed. I needed a fucking mirror so I could watch them sway with each thrust. Just imagining how she looked was enough. I was almost there, filling her with my release—

Fuck! "No condom. I gotta—"

"Don't!" She reached back and grabbed my ass, holding me in her. "I'm on the pill," she gasped. "Come in me."

Come in her. As if on command, I shouted her name while my body pumped into her. Her loud cry followed mine as she shook beneath me and clamped down so tightly she pulled everything from me. All I could do was wrap my arms around her and hold on.

Bethy

Tripp's lips grazed my back, and then he slowly pulled out of me before I collapsed on the bed, completely spent.

"Stay right here," he said softly. I wasn't sure where he thought I would go. It wasn't like I could move after that.

His smell was on the sheets pressed against my face, and my body tingled in response. Really? It was tingling? Already?

Tripp's hand was on my thigh. "Roll over," he said as he gently helped me move. I wanted to lie here with my face buried in his smell, but if he wanted me to roll over, I would.

He opened my legs and took the washcloth in his hand and began cleaning me up. Just like the first time. I watched him in awe as he touched me as if I would break. Once he was done, he lifted his gaze to meet mine. The possessiveness gleaming there startled me.

I had forgotten. Only Tripp. No one else had looked at me that way after sex. Ever. I had been an easy fuck for Jace in the beginning, but even after it all changed for us, Jace had never cleaned me up or stared at me like I was his reason for breathing.

Only Tripp. That look, I'd seen it before. Many times. I had just forgotten, or I'd refused to remember. Because once you knew that look, it was hard to accept less. The warm feeling that ran through me, making me feel cherished and special, was all because of that look.

He tossed the used cloth aside and crawled up to lie beside me, pulling me into his arms as he did. I couldn't talk yet. The emotion in my chest was all I could handle right now. This was why he could destroy me. This was why I built walls. Because being loved by Tripp changed you. His kind of devotion was rare. I knew that now. I hadn't known it then, and I hadn't known how excruciating it would be to lose this.

"I can't share you," he said as he pressed his mouth against my temple. "I know you want to take this slow, and you're scared. I get it. But I can't . . . this is mine. It always was. You were mine then, and you're mine now."

The idea of being with someone else after experiencing this again seemed impossible. I knew what shallow, meaningless sex was. I'd rather never have sex again if that was all there was. "I forgot, or maybe I couldn't allow myself to remember," I said as I lay against his chest.

"Forgot what?" he asked as he ran his fingers down my arm and then back up.

"You. How it is with you. I won't be able to move on from this. You've ruined me. I won't be able to forget again."

He took my arm and pulled me back so he could look down at my face. "What do you mean?" I had scared him. I could see that now. He didn't understand.

"I mean that nothing compares to having you inside me. I mean that when you treat me like I'm some special treasure that's all yours and give me that look of possession, I am ruined. How can I ever move on from that? I forgot once, but I won't be able to again."

He cupped my face with one of his big hands and brushed his thumb over my lips. "Are you telling me you won't be able to let anyone else touch your body?"

"Yes."

He closed his eyes tightly and inhaled sharply before his eyes opened back up and the green had darkened. "That's good, sweetheart. Because that means I don't have to go to prison for tearing a man apart for touching what's mine."

A giggle burst out of me, and he smiled, then bent down and captured my lips. It wasn't a hungry kiss. It was slow, delicious, and deep. I sank into his arms and decided I'd worry later about how I'd survive if he left me again.

⊞

When I opened my eyes this time, the sun was brighter outside, and I was in Tripp's bed alone. I much preferred waking up in his arms on the sofa. Stretching, I turned over and looked around his room, which hadn't changed much since the last time I was in here. The best thing about it was that it smelled like him. Snuggling in the Tripp-scented sheets was tempting, but I missed him being here with me.

I sat up and swung my legs off the big bed and grabbed a T-shirt he'd left lying over the chair in the corner. After pulling it on, I ran my hands through my hair and went to find Tripp.

The first thing I saw was his back. Even when he did something as simple as pour coffee, his back muscles moved. The sweats he'd pulled on hung low enough that I could see the dimples in his lower back and the cut of his hips. My hands itched to touch every inch of him. I really wanted to see his backside naked.

"You keep looking at my ass like that, and I won't give you this coffee I just made for you. I'll spread you open on the bar first and make you come again."

His mouth. I really liked his dirty mouth. "That's not much of a threat," I replied. I walked over to take the cup he was holding in his hand.

He slipped his other hand around my waist, cupping my bottom. "Glad you feel that way. Not sure you're getting out of here anytime soon."

As wonderful as being locked up with Tripp and having sex all day sounded, I had to be at the course by three. I was working the last shift of the day because I had worked so late last night.

"I have to go to work," I reminded him. "And you need to stop touching me while I'm holding hot coffee. I don't want to burn you."

He sighed and slipped his hand away. "When will you get off work?"

"Close to seven," I replied, then took a sip of the warm goodness in my cup.

He ran his hand through his hair and looked at the wall behind me for a moment. I knew he was thinking, and that made me nervous, but I drank my coffee and waited. We didn't have a definition for what this was we were doing. I had my own fears, and I knew he had his.

If I hadn't attacked him this morning after waking up to his hard cock pressing between my legs, then things wouldn't have escalated. Now that they had, we were going to have to reevaluate. This wasn't casual dating with sex. We had history. We had feelings and emotions already running deep, and then there was the way he looked at me after sex. All that made this a lot more.

"After this morning, I don't think I can be without you. I want you with me. I don't want space. I want you here. With me. All the fucking time. I want to be able to hold you when and where I want. I want to go to sleep and wake up with you in my arms. Bottom line, I need to know where we stand. Where's your head at?"

My head was still replaying the amazing sex we'd had. I wasn't ready to think past that. "I have to get ready and go to work. And you're right, we need to talk. But for now, can we just be us? No labels. Just us?"

He frowned. "Does being 'us' mean that if I want to grab you and kiss you in a public place or call you just to hear your voice, I can? And that you'll come sleep here with me every night?"

Sleeping with him every night was the one thing I wasn't sure of. I wasn't ready to depend on him. My questions about his plans for the future and his relationship with his parents still hadn't been answered. I wasn't sure he could answer all that now.

"Yes to everything but the sleepovers. I think for now, we should have a few boundaries. Lines we don't cross. Just to make sure we aren't moving into something we aren't ready for." Or that he wasn't ready for. He loved living on the road and moving from place to place. How long before he remembered that and resented me for being the thing holding him here?

He let his head fall back as he muttered a curse. He didn't like that line.

I set my cup down on the bar and slipped my arms around his waist. "It's not that bad. You just . . . you need to make sure this is the life you want."

"Sweetheart, you in my bed every night is exactly the life I want. I've wanted it since I was eighteen. I don't need to make sure of anything."

I so wanted to believe that. "Here's where we stand, Tripp. You didn't go to college, and you've only got experience as a bartender. I'm not sure how you're living without a job right now, unless you get paid really well to be on the board at the club. Me, I didn't go to college, and I'm a drink-cart girl at a golf course. We don't have any idea what our plans are for the future. I'm the girl from the trailer park who's used to grow-ing up living paycheck to paycheck, and you're the boy who was supposed to be the heir to the Newark legacy. But you ran from that life because you didn't want it. So here we are. Do you really want to get a job as a bartender in Rosemary Beach when your savings run out? I doubt that very much. And this condo isn't big enough to raise a family in, so when you get married, you'll need to get a house. We both know you can't afford a house here, so you would have to move." I stopped and felt panic rising in my chest. This was all the stuff I didn't want to think about. "All of that is why I need boundaries. I need to protect my heart some. Because when you leave here, because you will—you're meant for bigger things than being a bartender—I will be left here to pick up the pieces."

When I moved away from him, he let me go. I was afraid to look him in the eyes after that. He hadn't been thinking about any of it. He had been living in the now. I had just shown him the future.

I couldn't trust Tripp with my heart, because with him, it was forever. I didn't think about any of this with Jace. He had thought I wanted a proposal because I'd mentioned it once when I was drunk. But the truth was, I didn't plan the future with Jace. Deep down, I had expected him to leave me, too.

"You'd better get ready if you don't want to be late," Tripp said, breaking the silence.

My stomach sank, and tears stung my eyes. There were no reassuring words or even emotion in his voice. He wasn't even trying to convince me that there would be a chance with us. He knew I was right.

I stepped back and nodded without looking up at him, then hurried to his room to get the clothes in my bag and leave. I changed and threw the clothes from last night into my duffel. I would not cry. The pain in my chest would not shatter me. I was going to be OK. I was going to be OK. I was going to be OK.

He didn't move toward me to hug me or tell me good-bye. So I took his lead and went for the door. If what I had said pushed him away, then I was glad I knew it now. Because all I'd described was a list of scenarios. What would happen when we had to face those facts in reality?

"Why me, Bethy?" he asked, and I glanced back to see him standing in the hallway, watching me leave.

"What do you mean?"

"You didn't question any of this with Jace. You just lived in the present. I know he had no idea what he was going to do or what path he was going to take. He was living off his parents' trust fund and enjoying life, his degree unused. Yet you were his. You were happy and trusted that everything would be fine. So why me? Why do you need to know all this with me?"

I hated to say it out loud. Admitting it made me sound like I hadn't loved Jace enough, and that was never the case. I did love him. He just hadn't been my big love. I'd had that and lost it. After that, you can survive anything. "With Jace, I didn't worry about how I'd continue breathing if he walked out of my life. With you, I want it all. If I get a taste of what it could be, I won't ever want to let it go. I fell in love with you when I was sixteen, and that's never changed. But trusting you with my heart again is different. With you, I need to know it's forever."

I didn't wait for him to respond, and he didn't try to stop me as I opened the door and left.

Tripp

Woods leaned back in his office chair and smiled as he rubbed his chin. "I'd ask why, but I already know the answer. This is you putting down roots."

"It's time. I'm twenty-six years old," I replied.

"And there's Bethy," Grant added with an amused tone.

Yes. There was Bethy. She was the reason behind every decision I made.

"I know I've been preoccupied over the past year and a half, but how did I not know your grandfather passed away? I feel like a jackass," Grant said.

My mother's father, King Montgomery, had been a traveler. He rarely set foot in Rosemary Beach. He didn't believe in sitting behind a desk all day. He loved to see new places and experience new things. He'd had a heart attack on a hunting trip in Africa. I couldn't imagine seeing him suffer from an illness, bedridden. Knowing he died fast doing something he loved had made it easier to accept.

He and my father had never seen eye-to-eye. I think it was one of the reasons I loved the old man. He believed I should choose my own destiny. That was why he gave me the condo when I graduated from high school. I think it was his way of giving me a home to come back to if I did, in fact, choose to run.

"I wasn't back in Rosemary Beach yet. No one here knew him that well," I explained.

"Well, I think it's a great idea. I've played around with the thought more than once. But I never did anything because I have my hands full with the club. But I stand behind you. The property isn't technically for sale, but for you and for this, it is," Woods said.

I looked to Grant. I needed to hear his reply next.

"Heck, yeah. It's what I do. Bring it on. I love the idea," Grant said.

Standing up, I couldn't keep the grin off my face. "I want to move fast. I have to deal with some other things. I'll handle any extra cost to speed the paperwork along."

"No need. I'll make it happen fast."

Bethy

I stood at the door leading into the dining room. Tripp was in my section with a woman I didn't know. It had been five days since I walked out of his apartment. He hadn't called me, he hadn't texted, and until today, I hadn't seen him at the club.

In those five days, I had gone through the motions, but my heart wasn't in it. Last night, I had finally broken down and sobbed until I fell asleep. He had been so easy to push away. But then, hadn't he left me before and not looked back? When was I going to stop believing the man? Did he have to crush me over and over again first?

Jimmy was headed my way, and I backed up and waited around the corner, out of sight from the dining room.

"Chick's old. Like in her late forties old. He ain't hitting that shit. Something's up, but it ain't what you think. Wipe that pitiful look off your face and shake it loose, girl. Walk out there and strut your stuff, and show that man what he's missing. Don't act like he hurt you. Don't act like you miss him. And stop thinking he's on a date. Tripp's fine ass ain't messing around with that woman. Seriously, she could be his mom."

He was serious. I hadn't gotten close enough to see her. From the back, she had nice hair and legs. I couldn't tell about anything else. "Are you sure she's older?" I asked, praying he was right. If I walked out there and he was flirting with this woman, I was going to burst into a million pieces right in front of everyone. My heart could only take so much.

"Trust me, Bethy, it's not what you think. Swear it, baby. Go get their drink orders. And when you walk away, shake that ass. He'll be looking. You know how to strut. Do it." Jimmy winked and walked past me toward the kitchen.

I took a deep breath and prayed I didn't lose it out there and do something crazy, like cry. I could do this. Jimmy said she was older. Maybe she was a relative. Truth was, I did want to see him. I missed him.

Before I could get worked up again, I headed for the door and went to his table. He was talking and had a serious expression on his face. Almost as if he was discussing a business matter. Which made no sense. He didn't have any business matters.

His eyes glanced up, and he stopped talking as they locked on mine. He was surprised to see me working the dining room during lunch, since I didn't usually. He knew that. But there was also a hungry look there. Like he had wanted to see me as much as I wanted to see him. Which couldn't be the truth, because he hadn't called.

"What will you be drinking today?" I asked as I stepped up to the table. I was supposed to share the specials first, but my tongue was so tied I didn't even try.

I looked directly at the woman. She glanced at the menu she hadn't opened yet, then up at me. "Sparkling water for now," she replied. Jimmy was right. She was way too old for Tripp.

I turned my attention to Tripp, and he was still looking at me like I was his last meal. "Hey," he said simply.

What did I do with that? He'd ignored me for a week. I'd pushed him for answers about our future, and he'd backed away. Closed me off. Now this? "Hello, Tripp," I managed to get out.

"Uh, yeah, I'll have a Coke," he said. I nodded and turned to leave, and his hand closed around my arm. "Wait."

I couldn't make a scene in here, but I wanted to jerk my arm away and run. Turning back around, I noticed the lady beside him watching us with interest.

"Bethy, I want to introduce you to someone."

What? He was introducing me to the strange woman. Why? I wasn't sure what he wanted me to say to that, so I remained quiet.

He looked at the lady. "Quinn, this is Bethy. I mentioned her to you earlier. Bethy, this is Quinn. She's an interior designer. She does all the decorating here at the club," he explained.

OK. Odd. I nodded and smiled at her. I was sure she wasn't interested in being introduced to the help. Her smile, however, was very genuine. She held out her hand to me. "It's a pleasure to meet you, Bethy. Tripp's told me so much about you."

The surprise on my face was hard to mask. My emotions felt raw and open at this point, because he was making no sense at all. You would have thought I had just crawled out of his bed this morning and kissed him before coming to work. Not that I'd been completely ignored for five days.

I shook her hand and mumbled something before getting the hell out of there.

Jimmy was waiting for me with his hands on his hips as he peeked around the corner. "So who is it?" he asked.

"The interior designer Woods hires to decorate stuff, I guess. I have no idea what that was about. She acted like she knew who I was and shook my hand. I swear, Jimmy, I think I need to start taking anxiety meds. Tripp is fucking with my head, and I don't think I can take much more."

Jimmy pulled me into his arms and patted my back. "There, there, Bethy. I'm a pro at this. It's all gonna be OK. I've watched Blaire and Della go through this. Just hang in there."

I leaned back and looked at him. "Blaire and Della had men in their lives who worshipped the ground they walked on. This is so not the same."

Jimmy cocked an eyebrow at me. "Bethy, love, you need to snap out of it. Open your eyes, girl. That man is so obsessed with you he can't see straight."

If only.

I didn't argue with him. I walked past him and into the kitchen to get their drinks.

⌘

Tripp's eyes never left me. When I was in the dining room, they followed me everywhere. It was a miracle I hadn't dumped food on someone. I had taken their orders without making eye contact and refilled their drinks with a smile. By the time they were almost done with their meal, I was so tightly strung my head was hurting.

I massaged my temples and rested my head back against the wall. I didn't get off until six, and I could not afford a headache. When migraines hit me, I got sick. This could not happen. Not today.

"Lover boy paid, and he tipped you well. I grabbed it for you so they could clean the table.

Jimmy held up three hundred-dollar bills, which was ridiculous. I was not taking that much money. Their meal had only been a hundred dollars. I groaned and took the money and stuck it into my pocket. I would deal with him later, although I wasn't sure when that would be.

Tripp

She was upset with me. I knew she would be, but seeing it was hard. I wanted to grab her and haul her outside right then and tell her everything. But I had suffered five very long days without her to ensure that I never woke up again without her in my arms.

She wanted reassurance. She needed to know I was in this forever. Then that's what she'd get.

I had already started making plans for our future before she demanded to know what they were. But telling her my ideas was not the same as showing her I meant business.

The only way I let her walk out my door that morning was because she had said, *With Jace, I didn't worry about how I'd continue breathing if he walked out of my life. With you, I want it all.*

In that moment, I realized I wasn't her second-best. What we had was bigger than anything else she'd had. Even with Jace. Knowing I meant more to her was a game changer. I'd move fucking mountains to give her what she needed.

Looking back over the past five days, that was exactly what I did. Having friends in high places sure came in handy.

Bethy stepped out of the club's back entrance, and I straightened up from my relaxed stance on my bike. She didn't notice me until I was almost within reach. Her surprise quickly turned to anger. I bit back my grin. She was pissed at me. I would fix that soon. She'd demanded, and I was about to fucking deliver.

"What are you doing?" she asked, glaring at me.

"I know you're mad at me, but I need to show you something." I held out my hand to her. "A couple of somethings, actually."

She frowned and crossed her arms over her chest. "You're messing with my head, and I can't do this," she said, sounding tired.

I reached out and brushed the hair that had come loose from her ponytail out of her face. It gave me an excuse to touch her. "I'm sorry. But I swear, that's done. No more. Just come with me. Please?"

She looked like she was about to waver, so I decided to keep pushing.

"We don't have a far drive. Just give me ten minutes. I swear. It will explain everything."

I knew I'd won when her eyes looked back up at me. "OK."

I grabbed her hand and threaded my fingers through hers. "Let's take my bike," I said, leading her to where I had parked it.

I buckled the helmet on her head, even though I knew she could do it herself. Then she put her arms on my shoulders and climbed. When her arms wrapped around me, I closed my eyes and enjoyed the feel of her against me.

The drive was short, just to the outside of the club property. I took the small gravel path through the dunes and stopped just as we reached the hill overlooking the water. Shutting off my engine, I climbed off, then took her helmet and helped her off.

She looked around and then back at me with a frown. "What are we doing here?"

"The Kerrington Country Club owned this property. It was meant for expansion after Woods's father passed away, but Woods didn't go forward with it. So I bought it. All of it. I've hired Grant as the general contractor. I'm building a luxury hotel here so that those who don't want to purchase or lease a house during the summer months have another option. Hotel guests will have access to the Kerrington Club during the length of their stays." I paused. Her mouth dropped open, but she wasn't saying anything, so I kept going. "I met with Quinn today because I wanted to give her an idea of what I wanted and supply some different options. You'll be dealing with her from now own. She knows that you get the last call on everything."

Bethy held up a hand to stop me. "Wait, what? How did you afford this? A hotel is . . . big, Tripp. Really big."

I had forgotten that she didn't know everything. We had never discussed my money situation. I didn't realize it until she brought up my need to be a bartender and running out of money the other morning. "My mother's dad passed away two years ago and left everything to me. The rest of the family was upset, but the will was ironclad, and I was his only heir. When I came back to Rosemary Beach, this idea slowly started unfolding in my head."

"So you bought this land to build a hotel? Here? You're going to just . . . build one?" She was still staring at me in complete shock.

"You're here, Bethy," I replied, and then I took her hand

and walked her back over to my bike. "One more thing I need you to see," I explained. She didn't speak. She let me put the helmet back on her before we climbed back onto my bike so I could take her farther down the beach.

When I got to the spot that overlooked a long stretch of beach, I saw the blanket I had left earlier, along with the four lanterns at each corner to keep it from flying away and to give us some light. The sun had almost set. She stared as I took the helmet off and led her there.

"This is also property I purchased. It's got an amazing view and plenty of room to build as big a house as you want. Any house you want. We'll build it together."

"You want to build a house?" she asked in a whisper.

I watched as she looked around her, and then her eyes came back to me. "Yeah, I want to build a house. With you. One that you want. Whatever makes you happy, because as long as you're in it with me, I don't care where we live."

She continued to gaze up at me like I had lost my mind.

I reached into my pocket and pulled out the small velvet box.

When I went down on one knee, Bethy gasped. This was the part that scared the shit out of me. This was what I wanted. More than anything. But I wasn't sure she wanted it. Her words the other morning had led me to believe she did. She wanted forever with me. I did, too, and I hoped my actions showed that. No more dancing around each other, unsure of our future.

"You needed to know that what we had was forever. Bethy, it was forever with me when I was eighteen years old. You were all I could see then, and you're all I can see now. I've been waiting for you, sweetheart, to heal and to come back to me. But all you had to do was tell me you wanted forever, too. I would move heaven and earth to make that happen." I opened the box and watched her face. "Bethy Lowry, will you marry me?"

Silence.

I waited as she stared down at the ring in my hand and then back at my face.

"You did all this because of what I said?" she asked.

She was going to kill me. I managed a nod. "Yeah. I don't think you understand that if you asked me to fly to the moon and bring it back to you, I'd find a way."

She let out a soft laugh that turned into a sob, and my stomach knotted up. She wasn't supposed to cry. This was what she said she wanted. Then her head moved up and down as she let out another sob. "Yes."

No word had ever brought me more happiness. I was on my feet and pulling her into my arms instantly.

Her arms wrapped around my neck as I held her off the ground. She wasn't in heels, so she couldn't reach me.

"God, I love you so much. I swear, woman, I thought you were going to say no," I said into her neck as I closed my eyes and started breathing again.

"How you think any woman on earth could say no to you and a proposal like that, I don't know," she said, then sniffed.

"I missed eight years with you. I don't want to miss another day."

She pressed a kiss to my cheek, and I let her ease back down my body. I had plans for this blanket. "Can I have the ring now?" she asked sweetly. I realized I was still holding it in my hands.

Laughing, I opened the box back up and took the ring out. She held out her hand, and I slipped it onto her finger. I couldn't look away from the sight of it.

"Oh, wow, and I thought that possessive gleam couldn't get any worse," she said, smiling.

I tore my eyes off the ring to look at her face. My Bethy. "Just so we're clear, this means you either move in with me tomorrow or I burn down your apartment complex. You decide," I said, before tugging her down to the blanket with me. And placing her in my lap.

She threw back her head and laughed.

The sound that would never get old.

She looked back at me with a twinkle in her eyes. "Do I get morning sex every day?"

"And afternoon sex and shower sex and nighttime sex and hell, baby, even balcony sex," I assured her.

She laid her head on my chest. "I love you."

Bethy

Tripp's mouth touched my ear. "I need inside you. It's been five days of me remembering how fucking amazing that pussy is. Will you let me have you out here in the dark?"

As he asked, his hand slipped down the front of my shorts. I knew we were far enough away from other houses, but there was still the chance that someone could be out walking the beach. But then he slipped his finger inside me, and I decided I didn't care.

I moved off of him and started tugging down my shorts and panties. His eyes flared, and he moved his hands to the zipper on his jeans. "I swear, when we get home, I'll kiss every inch of you and take it nice and slow."

I straddled his lap, and he pulled out his hard length and held it as I lowered myself onto it.

"Fuck, that's hot," he growled.

If I wasn't so needy for him to fill me, I would have taken the time to tease him.

"There it is . . . yeah . . . sink down . . . fuuuuuck!" he roared as I slammed down onto him.

I threw back my head and cried out. I had known I was

ready for him, but I hadn't realized just how wet I was until he'd slipped in.

His hands grabbed my ass as I moved over him. "I'm going to lie back and let you ride," he said before crushing his mouth to mine. I moaned as his taste invaded me.

When he finally broke away, I shoved his chest back, and he laughed before lying back. I placed both hands on his chest and began to lift my hips up and down, panting as the sensation built. The pleasure I knew was coming.

"Pull your tits out, baby. I need to see them," he ordered in his husky voice that could make me do anything.

I pulled my shirt up and jerked my bra down so my breasts fell free.

"God, yes," he said as his hands cupped them gently before squeezing. Praises fell from his lips as he rolled my nipples in his fingers and watched my chest bounce. "So damn gorgeous," he whispered as he grabbed my hips and arched up into me.

"I'm gonna come," I whimpered, pressing down harder on him. "Harder, Tripp. I'm so close," I begged.

Tripp flipped me onto my back. "Open wide for me, sweetheart. Spread those legs, and let me sink into that sweet pussy. I'm ready to feel you come on my dick," he said, his voice thick with need.

That was all I needed. Tripp's dirty words sent me spiraling off, and I reached for him, crying his name as he lowered his mouth to my ear and told me just how wet I was and how sweet it smelled. When the second orgasm hit me, I was pretty sure I screamed.

My name tore from Tripp's lips just as his body jerked over me. My vision was blurred from the climax I'd had, but I watched my beautiful man as his mouth fell open and he filled me with his release.

When he was done, he wrapped me up and rolled onto his back, still buried inside me. "I think I'll just stay inside you all the time," he whispered against my hair.

Right now, I just might agree to that.

Tripp

I leaned against the doorframe of our bedroom, watching Bethy sleep. She was exhausted, but then, she'd also had six orgasms before I let her go to bed. Smiling, I took a drink of the water I'd gotten out of bed to get. She was here in my bed. My ring on her finger. I had pictured this moment for eight years.

She was my world.

Unable to stay away from her too long, I walked over and set my glass down on the nightstand. She rolled over, and her eyes fluttered. She yawned before looking at me. "I'm cold," she whispered sleepily. "Come keep me warm."

Smiling, I pulled back the covers and climbed in. "Always, baby. Always."

Read on for a look at the next novel in the Rosemary
Beach series featuring Mase and Reese . . .

When I'm Gone

Available from Atria Books in eBook and
trade paperback in April 2015

Prologue

Reese

"Come here, girl!" My stepfather's voice bellowed throughout the house.

Instantly, my gut twisted. The sick knot that came from being near him and knowing what he would do to me was a constant companion.

I stood up slowly from my bed and placed the book I was reading, or trying to read, down carefully. My mother wasn't home from work yet. She was supposed to be home by now. I shouldn't have come back from the library so early. A man and his young daughter had come up to me while I was looking through the children's picture books. He'd started talking to me and asking me my name. He'd wanted to know if I was getting a book for my little sister.

The embarrassment that came with that question reminded me of my stupidity, as always.

"GIRL!" My stepfather roared.

He was angry now. My eyes stung with unshed tears. If he would only just beat me like he used to, back when I was younger and I brought home poor grades in school. If he would just call me names and tell me how worthless I was . . . but he wouldn't. Once, I had wished more than anything that he would stop hitting me. I hated the belt, and the welts he left on my legs and bottom made it hard to sit down.

Then, one day he had. And I instantly wished he'd go back to hitting me. The bite from the belt was better than this. Anything was better than this. Even death.

I opened my bedroom door and took a deep breath, reminding myself that I could survive whatever he did. I was saving my money from the housecleaning jobs I had, and I would be leaving here soon. My mother would be glad I was gone. She hated me. She had hated me for years.

I was a burden on her.

I tugged my shirt down and tucked it into the shorts I was wearing. Then I pulled the shorts down so they covered more of my legs. It was pointless, really. I had long legs that were hard to cover up. There were never any shorts at the thrift store long enough.

It was only an hour before my mother got home. He wouldn't do anything that she could walk in on. Even if she did, I wondered if she would accuse me and say it was my fault. She had already blamed me for the way my body had changed four years ago. My breasts had grown too large, and she said I needed to stop eating, because my ass was fat. I had tried not eating, but it hadn't helped my bottom.

My stomach had flattened out, and it had only made my chest look larger. She'd hated that. So I had started eating again, but my stomach pudge never returned. One night when I had walked into the living room in a pair of cut-off sweatpants and a T-shirt to get some milk before I went to bed, she had slapped me and told me I looked like a whore. More than once she had called me a stupid whore who had nothing but her looks to get her anywhere in life.

I stepped into the living room to see Marco, my stepfather, sitting in his recliner with his eyes trained on the television and a beer in his hand. He had come home from work early.

His gaze swung to me and slowly trailed up my body, making me shiver with disgust. What I wouldn't give to be smart and flat-chested. If my legs were short and fat, then my life would be perfect. My face wasn't what attracted Marco. It was average enough. I just hated my body. I hated it so much.

Nausea crept up, and my heart raced as I fought back the tears. He loved it when I cried. It made him worse. I wouldn't cry. Not in front of him.

"Come sit in my lap," he ordered.

I couldn't do it. I had been able to avoid him for weeks by staying away from the house as much as possible. The horror of having his hands up my shirt or in my pants again was too much. I'd rather he kill me. Anything but this.

When I didn't move, his face twisted into an evil sneer. "Get your stupid, slutty ass over here and sit on my goddamn lap!"

I closed my eyes, because the tears were coming. I had to stop them. If he'd just hit me again. I'd take it. I just couldn't stand him touching me. I hated the sounds he made and the things he said. It was a never-ending nightmare.

Every second I stayed back was a second closer to my mother getting home. When she was here, he called me names but never touched me. She might wish I didn't exist, but she was my only salvation from this.

"Go ahead and cry, I like it," he sneered.

His chair creaked and then I heard the footrest slam down. I snapped my eyes open to see him standing up. Not good. If

I ran, I wouldn't make it past him. The only other option was the backyard, but his pit bull was out there. It had bitten me three years ago and I had needed stitches, but he hadn't let me go to the doctor. He'd told me to wrap it up; he wasn't putting his dog down over my stupid ass.

I had an ugly scar on my hip bone from the dog's teeth.

I'd never gone into the backyard again.

But watching him walk toward me, I wondered if being eaten by his dog wasn't better than this. It was a means to an end: death. Which didn't sound so bad.

Just before he reached me, I decided that whatever his dog did to me would be better than this. So I ran.

He cackled with laughter behind me, but I didn't let it slow me down. He didn't think I'd go out the back door. How wrong he was. I would face the pits of hell to get away from him.

But the door was bolted. I needed the key to unbolt it. No. No.

His hands grabbed my waist and pulled me back to feel his hardness pressing against me. The sour taste of vomit burned the back of my throat as I jerked away from him. "NO!" I yelled.

His hands moved around and grabbed my breasts and squeezed painfully. "Stupid whore. This is all you're good for. Couldn't graduate from high school because you were too damn stupid. But this body is meant to make men happy. Accept that, bitch."

The tears ran down my face. I hadn't been able to stop them. He knew the words to hurt me. "NO!" I cried out again, but this time the pain was there in my voice. It cracked.

"Fight me, Reese. I like it when you fight me," he hissed in my ear.

How could my mother stay married to this man? Was my father worse than this? She'd never married him. She never told me about him. I didn't even know his name. But no one could be worse than this awful man.

I couldn't do this again. I was done being scared. Either he would beat me until he killed me or he would kick me out. I had feared both for so long. Mother had told me once that all that men would do in this world was think about sex when they looked at me. I would be used by men my whole life. She constantly told me to leave.

Today, I was ready. I only had eight hundred and fifty-five dollars saved up, but I could get a bus ticket to the other side of the country and get a job. If I got out of this house alive, that's what I was doing.

Marco's hands slipped down the front of my shorts and I bucked against him, screaming. I didn't want his hand there. "Let me go!" I yelled loudly enough for the neighbors to hear.

He pulled his hand out and jerked me around by my arm so hard it popped. Then he slammed me against the door. His hand punched my face with a loud crack. My vision blurred and I felt my knees go weak. "Shut up, bitch, and take it."

His hands grabbed my shirt and jerked it up, then tugged my bra down. I sobbed, because I couldn't stop the horror. It was coming, and I couldn't stop him.

"Get away from my husband, you whore, and leave my house! I don't want to ever see your face again!" My mother's voice stopped Marco and he moved his hands off my breasts. I jerked my shirt back down.

My face was burning from the punch, and I tasted blood on my lip as the stinging cut under my tongue began to swell.

"OUT, YOU STUPID, GOOD-FOR-NOTHING WHORE!" my mother screamed.

That moment changed everything.

Mase

Two years later . . .

Fucking hell. What was that noise? I peeled my eyes open as sleep slowly faded away from my brain, and I was able to register what had woken me up.

A vacuum? And . . . singing? *What the fuck?*

I rubbed my eyes and groaned in frustration as the noise got louder. I was sure now it was a vacuum. And it sounded like a really bad version of Miranda Lambert's "Gunpowder & Lead."

My phone said it was only eight. I had been asleep for two hours. After thirty hours straight with no sleep, I was being awakened by bad singing and a motherfucking vacuum?

As she sang the first two lines of the chorus, I winced. She was getting louder as she sang. And it was seriously off-key. That was a good song she was butchering. Didn't the woman know you didn't come in people's houses at eight in the fucking morning and sing at the top of your lungs?

I was never going to get back to sleep with this racket.

Nannette must have hired an idiot to clean her fucking house. But then, knowing Nannette, she was pissed, because

I was here and there was nothing she could do about it. She probably paid the woman to screech outside my bedroom door. Nannette didn't own the house—our dad, Kiro, did. He'd told us that while she was in Paris I could stay in the house and spend some time with our other sister, Harlow.

This must be the bitch's way of getting me back for staying at her place.

Now she was singing the chorus over and over again at the top of her lungs. God, this was like waking to a nightmare. This woman so needed to shut up. I had to get some sleep before I went to visit with Harlow and her family. She knew I was here, and she was so excited about my coming to visit. But this idiot was messing my sleep up very effectively.

I threw back the covers and stood up and headed for the door before I realized I was naked. My head was pounding from lack of sleep, and this was just making me more angry as I searched the room for the damn jeans I had taken off when I'd gotten here. My vision was blurred and the dark curtains were closed. Fuck it. I reached for the sheet and wrapped it around my waist and went for the door.

I swung it open just as she started singing the opening lines to another song. Dammit. This time she was murdering "Cruise" by Florida Georgia Line.

I blinked and rubbed my eyes against the light, my vision still blurry. Shit, did the woman not see me here?

After a few seconds, I finally was able to open my eyes in a squint to see a round little ass wiggling as she bent over. My eyes slowly opened completely as I took in the longest damn legs I'd ever seen. And holy fucking hell, her ass. Was that a freckle or a birthmark under her left butt cheek?

She stood up, and the tiny waist only made her ass look

better. She continued to shake her bottom as she sang off-key. I winced as she hit a very high note, again off-key. Damn, the girl couldn't sing.

Then she turned, and I hardly had a moment to appreciate the front view before she screamed and dropped the vacuum cleaner as she pulled her earbuds out of her ears.

Big, round baby-blue eyes stared at me in horror as she opened and closed her mouth a few times as if she were trying to speak.

I took the moment of silence to check out her full pink lips and the perfect shape of her face. Her hair was pulled up in a bun, but it was the color of midnight. I wondered how long it was.

"I'm sorry," she managed to squeak out, and my eyes went back to hers. She was really something. There was an exotic quality about her. It was like God had picked all the best pieces and put them together to create her.

"I'm not," I replied. Not anymore. Who the hell needs sleep? Oh yeah. I do.

"I didn't know, uh , , , I thought the place was still empty. I mean, I didn't know someone was staying here. No car was outside, and I rang the doorbell but no one answered, so I used the code and came on in." She wasn't southern. Maybe midwestern. I just knew she wasn't from around here. She lacked the twang of most locals. There was a softness to her voice.

"I flew in. Had a car bring me here," I replied.

She nodded and then looked back down at her feet. "I'll be quiet. I can come back up and do this area later. I'll just go downstairs and start there today."

I nodded. "Thanks."

She barely glanced back at me, and her cheeks heated

as she let her gaze drop to my bare chest. Then she turned and hurried away, leaving the vacuum behind in her escape. I watched as she scurried away and enjoyed the way her bottom bounced. Damn, I hoped she cleaned several times a week. Next time I wouldn't be so exhausted. Next time I'd find out her name.

Once she was out of sight, I stepped back into the room and closed the door. A grin tugged at my lips when I thought about her face and how she realized I was only wearing a sheet. How did Nan have a housecleaner who looked like that? The girl was gorgeous.

I lay back down and closed my eyes. The image of that freckle sitting right there under the plumpness came to mind. I really wanted to lick that freckle. Cutest fucking freckle I'd ever seen.